Dear Reader,

For many years, Ha~~~~ ~~~~~~~~~
supporting and pro~~~~~~~~ ~~~~~~~~
to women, and celebrating women who make
extraordinary differences in the lives of others. The
Harlequin More Than Words program honors three
women each year for their compassionate dedication to
those who need it most, and donates $15,000 to each of
their chosen causes.

Within these pages you will find stories written by
Brenda Jackson, Stephanie Bond and Maureen Child.
These stories are beautiful tributes to the Harlequin
More Than Words award recipients, and we hope they
will touch your heart and inspire the real-life heroine in
you.

Thank you for your support. Proceeds from the
sale of this book will be reinvested into the Harlequin
More Than Words program so we can continue to
support more causes of concern to women. And you
can help even more by learning about and getting
involved with the charities highlighted by Harlequin
More Than Words, or even nominating an outstanding
individual in *your* life for a future award.

Together we can make a difference!

Sincerely,

Donna Hayes
Publisher and CEO
Harlequin Enterprises Limited

NEW YORK TIMES BESTSELLING AUTHOR

BRENDA JACKSON

BESTSELLING AUTHOR

STEPHANIE BOND

USA TODAY BESTSELLING AUTHOR

MAUREEN CHILD

Harlequin More Than Words:
ACTS OF KINDNESS

HARLEQUIN® MORE THAN WORDS

Recycling programs
for this product may
not exist in your area.

ISBN-13: 978-0-373-83795-3

MORE THAN WORDS: ACTS OF KINDNESS

Copyright © 2014 by Harlequin Books S.A.

Brenda Jackson is acknowledged as the author of *Whispers of the Heart*.
Stephanie Bond is acknowledged as the author of *It's Not About the Dress*.
Maureen Child is acknowledged as the author of *The Princess Shoes*.

This edition published by arrangement with Harlequin Books S.A.

For questions and comments about the quality of this book, please contact us at CustomerService@Harlequin.com.

Printed in U.S.A.

CONTENTS

STORIES INSPIRED BY REAL-LIFE HEROINES

NANCY SANDER

—Allergy & Asthma Network—
Mothers of Asthmatics

Nancy Sander, founder and president of the Allergy & Asthma Network Mothers of Asthmatics in Fairfax, Virginia, is trying to run out the door, take two telephone calls at once and, juggling it all, drops her calendar book and a set of files as she goes.

"I'm a mess," she says brightly. "I'm probably going to be senile before my time. Multitaskers tend to do too much."

The world needs more multitaskers like Nancy, though. Since she launched the grassroots non-profit organization back in 1985 in response to her daughter's battle with severe asthma and allergies, the AANMA has grown into an international network of families determined to overcome asthma and allergies rather than simply cope with them. Thirteen staff members and seventy outreach service coordinator volunteers offer support and practical strategies in twenty states while publishing monthly award-winning newsletters, magazines, books and other educational material. Above all, Nancy and the AANMA give hope to parents who thought they would have to struggle with their children's illness alone.

Nancy knows how important it is to feel supported.

For the first six years of her life, Nancy's daughter, Brooke, fought every day to live like other kids her age. She wanted to ride a bike, play basketball with her brothers, sleep through the night—and breathe. Brooke was born with life-threatening asthma and food allergies that routinely landed her in the emergency department and hospital, and out of school. Back in the early eighties, asthma wasn't well understood, and Brooke's doctors warned the family that the little girl would struggle all her life. Nancy believed them and structured her life around her daughter's asthma attacks.

"I did the best I knew how to do, but my daughter's symptoms didn't improve," she says now.

Nancy had no idea where to turn, and remembers clearly the time she stood in church, tears falling, as she tried to sing with the congregation the hymn, "It Is Well with My Soul."

"And I just said to God, 'No, this is not well with my soul. Why is Brooke so sick? I'm exhausted. I don't have the strength to do this. I don't know *how* to do this,'" she recalls. "But the strength I developed during those dark days still powers the work I do today."

It seems her plea for help was heard. When Brooke was accepted into a pharmaceutical clinical trial at Georgetown University Hospital, testing new methods of controlling asthma, life suddenly took a turn. Nancy and Brooke learned how to use a daily symptom diary and a peak flow meter, and Brooke started taking medication regularly, instead of waiting until she had an asthma attack. The regime worked, and after fourteen months, the family's dynamic changed. For the first time, Nancy could leave Brooke with a sitter for longer than an hour and cheer her sons on at their basketball games. For the first time, Nancy was out in the world again.

It was at these events that Nancy would overhear other parents complaining about their children's asthma symptoms.

"I'd listen to their descriptions and think, *This is a cakewalk. They're just not getting good care,*" she says.

Knowing she had to do something to spread the word about proper asthma and allergy control, Nancy fell back on her old skills as a freelance writer and started producing a short four-page newsletter to be left in her doctor's office. Next thing she knew, a local reporter wrote about Nancy's story.

The article ran on the day of Brooke's seventh birthday. As a houseful of kids ripped through the house, wearing high heels, dress-up clothes and jewelry, mothers, seniors, asthma sufferers and professionals from across the country started calling. They haven't stopped.

Nancy admits she never intended to start a non-profit organization, and if she'd known how much work would be involved, she might have been too intimidated to try. Luckily, ignorance is bliss, and Nancy has found hers in helping make a difference. Of course, most small miracles the organization accomplishes involve individual families, but sometimes Nancy thinks bigger. Much bigger.

Take the Asthmatic Schoolchildren's Treatment and Health Management Act of 2004, one of the last bills President George Bush signed before being re-elected. Some would say Nancy gave him no choice. AANMA called every day to remind his office how important the bill was. Finally, as he was thousands of feet in the air on Air Force One, he signed it. The bill protects the rights of children who must carry lifesaving asthma and allergy medication at school.

When Nancy heard that schoolchildren were suffering and others had died because their meds were locked away in school nurses' offices, she realized it was exactly the kind of fight the AANMA needed to tackle.

It was a period of her life she'll never forget, she says.

"Whatever comes into your life, no matter how negative or insurmountable it may seem at the time, it can have a positive impact," she claims.

Nancy, AANMA staff and dedicated supporters are still fighting seemingly insurmountable challenges to end suffering and death due to asthma, allergies and anaphylaxis. She wants to see the day when people who are diagnosed with asthma are treated the same way as those diagnosed with cardiac or brain concerns. Lungs are just as vital, she says, and everyone should have access to specialized care and appropriate medication. She's undaunted by the size and scope of this goal.

"There are very few impossible things," she says.

Meanwhile, Brooke is now a beautiful, accomplished woman, and Nancy couldn't be more proud of her. Because of her daughter, Nancy and AANMA are moving forward and lending a helping hand to millions of people diagnosed with asthma and allergies.

"I just get such a joy knowing that we can reach people with the information they need, knowing the impact it has on people every day," Nancy says. "I've been blessed."

For more information, visit www.aanma.org or write Allergy & Asthma Network Mothers of Asthmatics, 8201 Greensboro Drive, Suite 300, McLean, VA 22102.

BRENDA JACKSON

⌁WHISPERS OF THE HEART⌁

❦—BRENDA JACKSON—❦

Brenda Jackson is a die "heart" romantic who married her childhood sweetheart and still proudly wears the "going steady" ring he gave her when she was fifteen. Because she believes in the power of love, Brenda's stories always have happy endings. In her real-life love story, Brenda and her husband of many years live in Jacksonville, Florida, and have two sons.

A *New York Times* bestselling author of more than one hundred romance titles, Brenda is a recent retiree who now divides her time between family, writing and traveling with Gerald. You may write Brenda at P.O. Box 28267, Jacksonville, FL 32226, by email at WriterBJackson@aol.com or visit her website at www.brendajackson.net.

CHAPTER
~ONE~

"DAD, THE CATERER'S HERE. She's coming up the walkway." Paul Castlewood glanced up from the computer screen in his home office and looked into his daughter's smiling face, so like his own. Her slanted dark eyes were the only feature she had inherited from his ex-wife.

He closed the document file and began shutting down his computer. "Thanks, honey. Please show Ms. Chapman in."

Heather turned to leave. "And she's not bad looking either, Dad," she added. "Real pretty."

Paul shook his head. It wouldn't be the first time his daughter had tried to get him interested in a woman. He always found it amusing, because most literature he'd read said that when it came to single fathers, daughters were notorious for being territorial. Not true for his kid. She would marry him off in a heartbeat if she could.

But that wasn't going to happen.

He'd been married once and it had left a bad taste in his mouth. Heather had been barely five when Emma had decided she no longer wanted a husband or a child and had packed up her things and left. Her actions should have come as no surprise. She hadn't wanted a baby and had blamed him for her pregnancy.

Heather, who was now a few weeks shy of sixteen, had seen her mother only twice since she'd left, and sadly, the occasions had been the funerals of her maternal grandparents. Even eleven years later, Paul still couldn't understand how a woman could turn her back on a man who loved her and a daughter who needed her.

It had taken him long enough to stop trying to figure Emma out, and to just accept things as they were and move on. It hadn't been easy when juggling his job as a marketing analyst and that of a single father, but raising Heather on his own had been rewarding. His parents had helped out some in the early years, but since retiring six years ago they had become missionaries and spent most of their time in other countries.

He could hear the door open and the sound of his daughter's voice as she greeted their visitor. Michelle Chapman had come highly recommended as the best caterer in Lake Falls, and he was eager to have her take on Heather's birthday party.

He and Heather had moved from Atlanta to the quiet, historical Georgia town six months ago when the company he'd worked for had downsized, and he had accepted a nice buy-out settlement. Only a skip and a hop from Savannah, Lake Falls was everything he wanted. Even Heather hadn't complained about the move from the big city to a small town. She had quickly made new friends and had remarked a number of times that what she enjoyed the most was that he was around more often now that he'd set up his own website-design company at home.

He stood and crossed the room to glance out the window. Moss-draped oak trees lined the pretty cobblestone-paved street. He had stumbled across Lake Falls, a town many referred to as "Little Savannah," a couple of years ago when he had taken a detour off Interstate 95 during road construction. Like Savannah, the small, historic Southern town was the site of many famous Revolutionary and Civil War battles, and Lake Falls could also boast it was once the summer residence of noted novelist Louisa May Alcott.

The town was a step back into time. The old brick-and-stone homes had retained a lot of their original beauty and charm, and the local residents were so passionate about preserving these resplendent old buildings that an ordinance had been passed requiring city council approval for any new home construction in this section of town.

The house Paul had purchased, like the other homes on the street, had been built in the eighteenth century, with a wraparound porch and stately columns. He had fallen in love with it the moment the Realtor had shown it to him, and Paul considered it as one of the best investments he'd ever made.

As he walked out of the office, he could hear his daughter chatting excitedly with Ms. Chapman, something that didn't surprise him given the purpose of the woman's visit. Heather's sweet-sixteen party would be held here in their home with some of her friends from school and church. Deciding it was time to rescue the caterer before his daughter talked her to death, he hurried toward the living room.

When he rounded the corner to the foyer, he stopped dead in his tracks. Heather had been right. Michelle Chapman was a looker, and he had definitely taken notice.

"Ms. Chapman, this is my dad."

Michelle turned and met the eyes of the man who was leaning against the doorjamb and staring straight at her. She caught her breath when she felt a surge of something she hadn't felt in a long time. Physical attraction.

He was absolutely stunning. Tall—probably at least six foot two—and lean, with dark impressive eyes and caramel-colored skin, he was more handsome than any man had a right to be. He looked comfortable and at home in his bare feet, jeans and a T-shirt that accentuated his muscular physique.

She had heard through the grapevine that Paul Castlewood was absolutely gorgeous, but she had refused to believe the wild tales. Seeing was believing. The new guy in town was definitely hot. Michelle figured he must be in his later thirties, and as far as she was concerned, he was the epitome of male perfection.

"Dad, this is Ms. Chapman."

Heather's voice intruded on Michelle's thoughts and reality came crashing back. She was here because he needed a caterer for his daughter's upcoming birthday party. He was a client and therefore off-limits.

Putting on her professional face and wiping any inappropriate thoughts from her mind, she smiled and crossed the entryway as he shoved away from the door frame. She extended her hand. "Mr. Castlewood."

"Ms. Chapman. And I prefer that you call me Paul."

"And I'm Michelle."

"Got it."

He regarded her silently for a moment, not letting go of her hand. That gave her time to decide that the gold-rimmed glasses framing his dark eyes made him look ultrasexy versus brainy.

"We can meet in my office, Michelle," he said, finally releasing his grip.

"All right."

"Do you need my input?" Heather asked, smiling sweetly at her father and reminding them both that she was still there.

Paul rolled his eyes heavenward and then said, "Definitely not. I want to stay within the budget I've established. The menu is something Michelle and I can decide on, but I'll make sure you have the final okay."

"Fine by me, but if you change your mind…"

"I won't."

"But if you do," Heather said, grinning, "I'll be in the kitchen working on my biology project." She turned and sashayed toward the back of the house.

Michelle glanced up at Paul and he smiled. "Sometimes I wonder why I keep her around," he said jokingly.

"Because you love her," Michelle said easily. That was how things had been between her and her own dad. They'd had a special relationship. In Michelle's eyes, Prentiss Chapman had been everything a girl could want and need in a father, and even now, six months after he'd passed away, she was still trying to get over her loss.

"Yes, that I do," Paul responded, directing her down a long hall. "She's a good kid. She works hard, makes good grades in school and is respectful. However," he added as they entered his office and he turned to face her, "on the downside, she will talk your ear off if you let her."

Michelle couldn't help but laugh. "Have you lived in Lake Falls long?" he asked, offering her a chair. She glanced around. The office, like the rest of the house that she'd seen so far, was tidy and neat. There was no clutter anywhere.

"All my life, except for the time I moved away to attend college, then worked in Memphis for a few years. In fact, I grew up in a house right around the corner from here."

"Your parents still live there?"

"No. My mom died eight years ago while I was away at college, and my father died six months ago."

"I'm sorry for your loss."

"Thanks." She felt there was no need to go into any details about why she had turned down the promotion of a lifetime at the corporation in Memphis where she'd worked to return home to take care of her ailing father. How could she explain that those two years together had been both uplifting and sad?

"I didn't expect you to be so young."

At his appraising glance, she felt a warm rush of blood through her veins. She was attracted to him and that wasn't good. She found herself struggling to remember that this was a business meeting. "I'm here to break the myth that only older women know how to cook these days."

"So who taught you how to cook?"

"My grandparents. They owned a restaurant in town for years and I worked for them. That's where I learned to peel my first potato."

"Do you mind if I asked how old you are?" he asked.

She wondered why he wanted to know but answered anyway. "Twenty-eight." Deciding they needed to begin talking business, she said, "I have a couple of suggestions for your daughter's party."

"Okay, what are they?"

Opening the folder she was carrying, she placed

several colorful documents on his desk and pointed at one. "This popular treat is called a pizza porcupine and will serve as part of the main course. The number of teens you're inviting and whether the majority are boys or girls will determine how many I need to make. Guys tend to have bigger appetites."

"I wouldn't doubt that," Paul agreed. He had meant to go over a guest list with Heather last week. However, she had been a little under the weather after coming down with a slight cold. She was feeling better now but was trying to play catch-up with that science project.

"I'll double-check with Heather to determine the number of friends coming. It'll be less than twenty, I would think."

Michelle nodded. "Here are some other choices I'd suggest, because they're usually big hits. Hamburgers and hot dogs are always popular with teens, and chips are a favorite with practically any kind of dip."

"Everything looks good," Paul said as he scanned the papers.

"My job is to make sure it tastes good, as well. Once you give me the go-ahead, I'll come up with a menu that I think will work and present it to you by the end of the week. And I suggest you do run it by Heather. She'll know what her friends like."

"That sounds wonderful. I've hired Ravine Stokes as party planner. She'll be responsible for working out the music and games."

Michelle smiled. "Ravine is a high-school friend of mine and she and I have worked together on a number of projects. By the time they finish all the activities she'll have lined up for them, they'll be ready to eat. And I'll make sure they have lots of snack foods when they first arrive. I'd like to drop off some sample treats tomorrow."

"You don't have to do that. You came highly recommended by both Ravine Stokes and Amy Poole. And I understand Ms. Amy's word is gospel in this town."

Michelle chuckled as she stood. In a way, she was grateful the meeting with Paul was coming to an end. She found it hard sharing the same space with him. "It is. Ms. Amy has been around forever and has made herself a spokesperson for the town's welcoming committee."

He was about to open his mouth and say something when his brows drew together in a worried frown and he quickly got to his feet. "Heather! Baby, what's wrong?"

Michelle turned in time to see his daughter stumble into the room, gasping for breath. Michelle immediately recognized the signs of an asthma attack, since she had suffered from a number of them throughout her childhood. She rushed out of her seat and made it to Heather's side the same time her dad did.

"Get her inhaler," she ordered, starting to loosen Heather's blouse.

"What?" Paul asked in a frantic voice as he helped his daughter to the sofa. "She doesn't have an inhaler. She hasn't had an asthma attack in years, not since she was around five. She outgrew her asthma."

Michelle glanced up at him. It was obvious he didn't know that a person didn't outgrow asthma. "Grab my purse." She pointed to the chair where she'd been sitting. "We can use my inhaler."

For a split second she could sense Paul Castlewood's hesitation, and then, as if he'd decided to trust her with his daughter's life, he did as she asked. Michelle continued to hold the young woman, who was still fighting for breath.

"Everything is going to be fine, Heather," she said softly. This attack was relatively mild compared to others she'd seen. Her own, when she did have them, tended to be more severe. But Michelle knew mild attacks could quickly become life threatening, and was taking no chances.

"Here." Paul thrust her purse into her hands. She pulled out her inhaler and immediately sprayed four puffs into the air. It was now primed and ready to deliver a full dose. "Relax, Heather. Try breathing out gently. We need to empty your lungs as much as possible."

Luckily, the teen was calm enough to follow orders.

"That's right," Michelle said, putting the inhaler in place. "Now I want you to start breathing in slowly and as deeply as you can."

"I don't understand," Paul said. "Heather doesn't have asthma. Why is she having an attack?"

It wasn't until then that Michelle realized just how

close he was standing beside her. She turned her head and looked directly into his eyes. "It's quite obvious, Paul. She does have asthma."

His expression was one of disbelief. "But that's not possible. Like I said before, she had asthma as a child but over the years she's outgrown it."

Michelle shook her head. "You never outgrow asthma. It stays with you for life. Symptoms may go away for long periods of time and then come back when something triggers it again, like right now."

"Something like what?"

Michelle quickly assessed Heather. The girl was breathing more deeply now, though she still looked frightened. Michelle gave her shoulder a reassuring squeeze before turning back to Paul.

"Several things. Pollution, changes in the weather, allergies, colds or flulike symptoms, and—"

"She had a cold last week. But she's had them in the past and this has never happened. That doesn't make sense."

Michelle wished she could explain to him that nothing about asthma really made sense. It was a condition that affected more than fifteen million people in North America, and was the primary reason for most hospital stays. One good thing was that it could usually be controlled enough that a person could live a normal and active life…as she was trying to do.

"I know it might not make sense, but the effects of asthma are real. Heather's symptoms could have been much more serious if not treated early. Ordinarily I would never share my inhaler, but this was an emergency."

Paul lifted a brow. "How long have you had asthma?"

Michelle shook her head. "I don't recall a time that I didn't have it. And because I know how serious asthma can be, I'm a member of AANMA, Allergy & Asthma Network Mothers of Asthmatics. It's a national organization, and I'm part of their network and I volunteer as an outreach service coordinator. In fact, I'm taking a truckload of materials to various elementary schools in town."

Heather made a move to stand up and Paul and Michelle backed away a little. Michelle almost stumbled and he automatically reached out and grabbed her around the waist. Again she felt a rush of warmth at his touch. "Thanks."

"Don't mention it."

She glanced up at him, fully aware that his arm was still around her waist.

"Sorry, Dad."

Paul dropped his arm from Michelle and slipped it around his daughter. "There's nothing for you to apologize for, honey. How do you feel?"

A shaky smile touched Heather's features. "Better. It was scary. One moment I was coughing and the next I felt like I couldn't breathe."

Paul glanced at Michelle before turning his attention back to his daughter.

"That hasn't happened in years," Heather said. "I probably just got overworked doing that project. And the smell of those markers I was using almost took my breath away. That's probably what did it. I don't think it had anything to do with asthma."

Michelle shook her head. "Paul, I suggest that you take Heather to a doctor tomorrow just for a checkup. There are a number of medications for the treatment of asthma and they can—"

He didn't let her finish. "Thanks for the advice, and I appreciate all your help, but I think I can take things from here."

It was obvious to Michelle that he wanted her to leave and wasn't open to anything she had to say regarding his daughter. "All right. I'll contact you about the party menu."

She glanced down at Heather and smiled. "I'm glad you're doing okay now."

The girl returned her smile. "Thanks for being here, Ms. Chapman."

"You're welcome." She turned to Paul, but he was looking at his daughter. "I know my way out."

MICHELLE HAD MADE IT to the front door when Paul called her name. She wanted to keep walking, but then remembered he was a new client and she needed the business. "Yes?" she said, swinging around to watch him approach. Once again a tingling sensation swept through her. Once again she thought that he was a very good-looking man. "Was there something else you wanted?" she asked when he came to a stop in front of her.

"You can't go anywhere without these," he said, holding up her car keys.

"You're right, I can't." She reached out to take them from him.

He handed them over easily and then seemed to hesitate. "About what happened in there…"

"Yes?"

"I appreciate you coming to Heather's aid, and I know you believe you're absolutely sure about this asthma thing, and her not outgrowing it. But I beg to differ. You heard her yourself. She probably got a whiff of those markers she's been working with and it got to her. I'm thinking it was probably nothing more than an allergic reaction."

Michelle was convinced otherwise but knew it was best not to argue with him. "Just do me a favor and take her to the doctor for a checkup to be on the safe side. She really needs her own inhaler."

He leaned against the doorjamb. "So now in addition to being a caterer, you're also a social worker who gives family advice, as well?"

"No, I'm only a caterer," she said, again hearing a sting in his tone. "One who has asthma. Goodbye, Paul."

She opened the door and walked out.

CHAPTER
⌁—TWO—⌁

"So WHAT DO YOU think of Mr. Castlewood?" Michelle closed the oven door and glanced up at the elderly woman who was sitting at her kitchen table sipping a cup of tea. Amy Poole had turned eighty-two her last birthday, and years ago the mayor had declared May 1 of every year as Amy Poole Day in Lake Falls. It was an appropriate honor for a woman whose ancestors had been among the town's founders.

"He's okay, I guess," she responded in a nonchalant manner.

"Just okay? You mean he didn't make your heart go pitter-pat?"

Michelle smiled, deciding she would definitely not admit the man had done a little more than that. It had taken a trip to the grocery store, as well as a couple of hours of working outside in her yard yesterday, to get her heart rate back to normal. The man had rattled her in more ways than one.

"Yes, just okay. He's definitely a person who doesn't like anyone getting into his business."

Ms. Amy's brow wrinkled. "Why do you say that?"

Michelle decided to tell her about the incident involving Heather.

"My word," Ms. Amy said in alarm. "That child doesn't have an asthma-management plan?"

Michelle smiled sadly. "No. And I honestly think he believes a person can outgrow asthma. It's like he's determined to block anything I say regarding the matter out of his mind. But I'm hoping that he takes her in to see the doctor for a checkup like I suggested. I would hate for her to be caught unawares again."

"So other than disagreeing on his daughter's condition, everything is fine between the two of you?"

Michelle raised an eyebrow. Ms. Amy was talking as if they were a couple. "If you're asking if I was hired to be the caterer for his daughter's birthday party, then the answer is yes. Thanks to you and Ravine, I got the job."

Michelle placed another tray of cookies in the oven.

"But you do think he's good-looking?" her visitor asked.

Michelle's heart jolted in her chest at the thought of just how good-looking Paul Castlewood was. But by the end of their conversation yesterday, she had dismissed the image from her mind and replaced it with one of a grouch.

"Yes, he's handsome, but you know what they say. Beauty is only skin-deep."

"Yes, that's true, but I had the privilege of holding conversations in church with Mr. Castlewood, and found him to be a very nice man."

Michelle laughed as she joined Ms. Amy at the table. "He would be nice to you, since you're old enough to be his grandmother."

"And you, young lady, are young enough to drum up some interest where he's concerned."

Michelle frowned. It sounded as if Ms. Amy was trying to play matchmaker. She certainly hoped not, but just in case, figured she should set the record straight. "I'm a woman with good eyesight, so there's no way I'm going to sit here and pretend I didn't notice how attractive Paul Castlewood is. However…"

"Hmm, sounds like a big *however.*"

"It is. However, the man rubbed me the wrong way yesterday."

"Is that why you baked all these treats for him today?"

She'd wondered how long it would take Ms. Amy to mention that. "I only baked them because I wanted him to have a sample of what I can do."

"I told him what you could do. He doesn't need any samples. What the man needs is a good woman to mend his broken heart."

Michelle had been up since the crack of dawn, and it was nearing noon. She didn't have the strength to argue. Besides, it wouldn't do any good. Amy Poole was convinced that what she was saying was true. "In that case, you should have sent Wanda Shaw his way." Wanda worked at the local post office. "She's looking for a husband."

Ms. Amy released a snort. "Wanda is looking for someone to take care of her so she won't have to work again. She and Mr. Castlewood aren't right for each other."

"But you think that he and I are?"

"Yes."

With a heavy sigh, Michelle got up from the table. In her heart she knew that Ms. Amy wanted what was best for her, but she just couldn't figure out why the older woman thought she would be interested in Paul Castlewood or vice versa. "I didn't bake these just for him, you know."

"You didn't?"

"No. I plan to stop by the children's hospital and drop a few batches off there."

"That's kind of you."

Michelle smiled. "I'm a kind person."

Ms. Amy chuckled. "Yes, you are, which is why I think you and Mr. Castlewood would get along nicely."

PAUL PARKED HIS CAR under a moss-draped oak tree and studied Michelle Chapman's business card. He had thought about calling her, but knew that wasn't good enough, especially after the way he'd treated her yesterday. She deserved a personal visit.

After Heather had taken a nap, she had been her old self. Convinced his daughter had had a possible allergic reaction instead of an asthma attack, he had thrown out those colored markers she had been using and gone to the store to purchase the unscented kind.

He had waited until after lunch today to drive over to Michelle's. He glanced around now as he strolled up the brick-paved walkway. Michelle had an older house with a large veranda. He was immediately taken by her picturesque flower garden, as well as her home's stately entranceway. The neighborhood, like his, oozed Southern beauty and charm.

When he reached her door, part of him wondered why he was really paying her a visit. She had indicated that she would be contacting him to provide him with a sampling of her cooking. He could have waited to have this conversation with her then. Why was he determined to see her now?

He would be the first to admit that although he had gotten a bit annoyed with her yesterday, he had appreciated that she was a good-looking woman. And each time their gazes had connected he had felt his pulse rate go up. Her face, the color of chocolate, was a perfect round shape, and her dark brown hair fell like soft waves around her shoulders, giving her a radiant look. Still, he couldn't help wondering how one woman could have piqued his interest so easily.

He heard the sound of footsteps within seconds after ringing the doorbellz and saw the surprise on her face when she opened the door to find him standing there.

"Paul? Is something wrong? How's Heather?"

"She's fine. May I come in?"

"Sure," she said, stepping aside. "Is there anything I can get you to drink?"

He shook his head. "No, I don't plan to be here long. I just wanted to thank you for yesterday."

"You've thanked me already."

"Yes, but I also felt I was a little abrupt at the end. My only excuse is that I was shaken by what happened and wasn't open to any suggestions or comments about what might have been wrong with my daughter."

She nodded. "I understand," she said softly.

"So will you accept my apology?"

She smiled. "Yes, apology accepted."

Feeling better about things, Paul glanced around the living room. He liked her taste in furniture and decorating, and took the time to tell her so.

She seemed pleased. "Thanks. Are you sure you don't want anything to drink?"

"I'm sure. Besides, I don't want to take you from your work."

She waved off his words as she led him toward the kitchen. "You won't be. In fact, you arrived at the right time. I was just taking some nutty cheese bars out of the oven."

He chuckled. "Mmm, smells good."

She glanced over her shoulder at him. "I'm glad you think so, since it's one of the options for Heather's party."

"Is that a fact?"

She couldn't help but smile. "Yes, it is a fact."

When they reached the large kitchen, Paul was surprised at how well used it was, but still neat. His kitchen had a tendency to look like a war zone by the time dinner was served.

"Your kitchen is huge, but welcoming," he said, taking a seat at the table while she walked over to a double oven.

"Thanks. Now, this is my final offer. Are you sure you don't want even a coffee? I brew a mean cup."

He lifted a brow. "How mean?"

"My dad swore it could grow hair on his chest."

Paul laughed. "In that case, I think I'll try one."

Michelle went about preparing coffee, trying not to notice that today, just like yesterday, he had that at-home look. The only difference was that he was in her house and not his. But still, there was something about him in well-worn jeans, a T-shirt and a pair of Nikes that would probably make him look relaxed and at home wherever he was.

"So how long have you had your catering business?"

She shifted sideways and noticed that he was watching her. She was glad she looked fairly decent this morning in a tailored blouse and capris, although her hair was up in a ponytail.

"I've had it a few months. When I lived in Memphis, I worked as a manager for an accounting firm."

"What happened?" he asked. "You get zapped with corporate burnout?"

She smiled sadly. "No. When I left Memphis, I chose the profession of caretaker."

At the curious look that flashed in his eyes she explained. "The doctor gave my father less than a year to live and I wanted to be with him for every single second that he had left. So I turned in my resignation, packed all my belongings, leased out my home and headed here. Like you, my father was a single dad. But unlike you he was a widower instead of a divorcé."

"And how do you know I'm a divorcé? I don't believe my marital status ever came up in any of our prior conversations."

Michelle swallowed, hoping she hadn't put her foot in her mouth. But she figured she would be honest with him. "You're new to our town, so most of us know everything about you…at least everything you told Ms. Amy."

He looked incredulous. "You mean, she was pumping me for information?"

"Afraid so." Although Michelle smiled, she couldn't help but feel bad for him at the moment. He honestly hadn't had a clue, and probably thought Ms. Amy had been conversing with him because she was a friendly old woman. Of course, that was true, but everyone in Lake Falls knew Amy Poole, who had been married to her childhood sweetheart for over sixty years before he'd passed away a few years ago, was a romantic at heart and enjoyed playing Cupid.

Michelle just hoped their conversations earlier that morning had made the older woman put away her bow and arrow, because she had no intention of getting struck. Just like any other woman, Michelle wanted to meet a nice guy and get married, but now was not a good time. She needed to put all her energy into getting her business off the ground rather than investing in a relationship that might not go anywhere. She'd done that before with Lonnie Fields. They had met at a business workshop, and after dating her for two years, he'd decided to leave her behind without looking back when his company transferred him to the West Coast. The only reason she hadn't succumbed to a broken heart was because she had begun to have doubts anyway.

Upon seeing the guarded look on Paul's face, she said, "Hey, don't take it personally. In fact, she genuinely likes you and wanted to get to know you. However, at the same time she was sizing you up to see which of the single ladies in Lake Falls was best suited to meet your needs."

He didn't say anything for a moment and then asked, "So who is this unlucky lady?"

As Michelle poured the coffee, she thought about lying and saying she had no idea. But the truth of the matter was that she did, since Ms. Amy had practically come out and told her. And since Michelle felt sure nothing would ever come of the older woman's shenanigans, he had a right to know.

She placed the cup of coffee in front of him, met his gaze and said, "Yours truly." At the lifting of his dark brows she added, "I'm the unlucky lady."

CHAPTER
～THREE～

PAUL HOPED HE HAD heard her wrong. But staring into Michelle's face and seeing her apologetic expression, he knew he had not. He also knew that she was an unwilling victim of Amy Poole's mischief as much as he was. He couldn't help but recall the last time he had been targeted in an older woman's matchmaking scheme. His grand-aunt Zelda had decided he should remarry when Heather had turned ten, saying his daughter needed a female influence in her life.

Aunt Zelda had given a dinner party, the likes of which he would never forget. She evidently had erroneously put out the word that her divorced and well-off nephew was up for grabs. That night, women at the party had flocked around him as if he was the last man on earth. Some had openly flirted, while others had decided to go straight into seduction, regardless of the fact they had an audience. He had sworn he would never let another person place him in such a situation again.

He studied Michelle's features. She was evidently waiting for him to say something. Give some sort of indication that he'd heard and understood what she'd said.

"So you're looking for a husband?" he asked.

The expression that appeared on her face told him her answer before she opened her mouth. "No."

The fierceness of her tone confirmed it. He believed her, but just to set the record straight, he said, "Good, because the last thing I'm interested in is a wife."

He saw how relieved she looked and automatically lowered his guard. It was just as he'd suspected. She was no more interested in marriage than he was. He knew his reasons, and couldn't help wondering about hers, but was too much of a gentleman to ask. Besides, it really wasn't any of his business.

He took a sip of his coffee as she went back to the oven to take care of whatever she was baking. Moments later she slid one of the pastries onto a plate and then walked back again. It smelled tantalizing and he almost licked his lips as he picked up the fork and took his first bite, after waiting a moment for it to cool.

His reaction wasn't slow in coming. The nutty cheese bar was the most delicious pastry he'd ever eaten. He quickly told her so and was rewarded with her smile. And that smile, which seemed to stretch from one corner of her mouth to the other, did something to his insides.

"Thanks," she said, going back over to the sink. "I figured on making a number of these as part of the menu. Now, as for the cake, since you mentioned Heather likes strawberries, I've decided to bake one with a strawberry filling."

"She's going to love that," he said, taking another bite of the pastry. "And I have her working on that list of invitees so we'll know how many are coming."

He watched as Michelle kept herself busy at the counter, and couldn't help wondering if it was intentional. "Won't you stop a moment and join me in a cup of coffee?"

He could tell his question surprised her, and she took a few moments before responding. Then, tossing aside a dish towel, she said, "Yes, I think I will. You can tell me what the doctor said about Heather."

Paul felt himself getting annoyed again, just as he had yesterday. He was grateful that Michelle was concerned about his daughter's welfare, and he'd appreciated her timely intervention, as well as the information about the asthma organization she volunteered for. But Heather was his responsibility and no one else's. Besides, she was due for a routine physical next month and he would mention to the doctor what had happened then.

He glanced at his watch. "You know, I hadn't realized it had gotten so late. I need to leave." He rose to his feet.

"But what about those treats I baked for you to

sample? If you wait a minute I'll pack them up for you and Heather."

It was the least he could do after she had taken the time to do all that baking. "Okay, I'll wait."

MICHELLE PACKED UP a sampling of her baking and watched Paul out of the corner of her eye. He was standing at her kitchen window, staring out. It was plain to see that he was agitated about something. Asking what the doctor had said about Heather had hit a nerve with him for some reason. She had picked up the same attitude yesterday. She could only assume that although he had dropped by to apologize for his abruptness the day before, he still didn't like her butting her nose into his family's business.

"Here you are," she said, handing him the container of baked goods. "I hope you and Heather enjoy them."

He moved away from the window and crossed the kitchen floor. "I'm sure we will."

"And I still plan to have a menu ready for you at the end of the week. If you approve it, then we can go ahead and finalize numbers."

"That will be fine."

Something pushed her to say more, and she hoped her words would smooth the waters between them. "Contrary to what you might think, Paul, I'm not a busybody. My concern for Heather is genuine. I like her. It would be hard not to. She's a wonderful girl. You've done a fantastic job raising her."

She could tell her statement had caught him off

guard, and for a while he said nothing. At last he replied, "I appreciate you saying that."

"Well, it's true. I'll see you out now."

He walked beside her as they headed for the front door. When they reached it, he said, "Thanks for everything. I'll call you later this week with the exact number of kids who will be attending the party. The RSVPs should all be in by Thursday."

Michelle merely nodded and opened the door. He gave her a slight smile before walking out of the house, and she silently closed the door behind him.

WHEN MICHELLE HEARD the sound of Paul's car pulling out of her driveway, she leaned against the closed door and squeezed her eyes shut, thinking she liked him a whole lot more than she really should. When it came to his daughter he was overprotective, but hadn't her own father been the same way?

She had practically never spent a night away from home when she was growing up because her father had been afraid she would have an asthma attack while he wasn't there. When she was sixteen, he'd finally relented and allowed her to attend Misty Edwards's sleepover party, only because Ms. Amy had pleaded with him to do so.

Michelle's thoughts shifted back to Paul. Regardless of whether either of them wanted to admit it or not, from the moment they had met there had been an attraction. And although they had agreed today that neither was interested in marriage, that hadn't stopped a heated desire from working its way through her body. And just now, when she'd walked him to the door, she'd had a feeling he wanted to kiss her.

As she headed back toward the kitchen, she was glad he hadn't. All she and Paul shared was a business relationship, and it would be wise for her to remember that.

HE HAD WANTED to kiss her.

And the very thought of doing so was flooding his senses to the point he couldn't think straight. When she had walked him to the door, he had stood there, breathing in her scent, taking in her beauty and appreciating her caring nature. Although she wasn't interested in marriage any more than he was, she would make some man an exceptional wife.

The words she had spoken about his part in Heather's upbringing had touched him. He had recognized early on that being a single father wouldn't be easy, and if his in-laws had had their way he never would have gotten the opportunity to try. For some reason they'd felt it was their right to raise Heather after Emma had walked out, and that he couldn't go it alone. He had proved them wrong.

He didn't want to dwell on the past, but remembering those times made him appreciate how things were now.

As Paul parked in front of his house, he could see Heather on the porch, leaning against a column and talking to a boy named Jason. Paul couldn't help noticing that Jason had begun hanging around a lot lately. Heather claimed they were just friends, but Paul was beginning to wonder.

His daughter's face lit up in a smile when she turned and saw him; however, Jason was ready to crawl under the porch. The kid always seemed nervous around him, and Paul smiled, thinking that was a good thing.

"Dad, got anything for me?" Heather asked, leaving Jason standing on the porch as she raced over to him.

Paul chuckled. Nothing had changed. She'd been asking him that since the time she was able to talk.

"I stopped by Michelle's house and she sent some baking for us to sample," he answered.

"Wow! That's cool!"

He glanced at the youth. "Hello, Jason."

The young man smiled hesitantly and waved his hand. "Hello, Mr. Castlewood."

"And how are you?"

"Just fine, sir."

"And your parents?"

"They're fine, too. Do you need help getting anything out of your car?"

"No. But thanks for asking." Paul hated admitting it but Jason wasn't such a bad kid. He had good manners, was respectful and didn't have any tattoos or piercings…at least not in plain sight.

"So you saw Ms. Chapman again?" Heather's excitement couldn't be missed.

"Yes, I saw her."

"That's good." She was almost beaming.

"And why is that good?"

"Because I think she's nice. I like her."

He chuckled again. "You just met her yesterday."

"It doesn't matter."

He studied his daughter, wondering just what she meant.

Both Heather and Jason dived into Michelle's baking as if it were the last food they would eat. They sang her praises while gobbling down a huge portion of the treats, along with tall glasses of milk. A few hours later, before Jason left, he drummed up enough courage to ask if Heather could go to the movies with him the weekend following her sixteenth birthday.

Paul didn't have a good reason to turn him down, especially since he'd told Heather she could begin dating once she turned sixteen. He realized his little girl was growing up, and one day he wouldn't be the most special man in her life, which meant he really needed to start getting a life of his own. His position on marriage hadn't changed, but there was nothing wrong with having a female friend, someone to date on occasion, who wasn't clingy. He'd dated a few clingy women in the past. They'd thought they could storm into his life and become the center of his world, replacing Heather and his common sense. He had proved time and time again that wasn't possible. He couldn't ever see himself letting go and losing control with any woman.

Except possibly Michelle.

There was something about her that had caught his attention from the first. And the remarkable thing was that she hadn't been trying. He could understand why Heather had immediately liked her. The thought of her giving up her career to care for a dying parent touched him.

As Paul slid between the covers that night, visions of Michelle danced in his head, and he wasn't sure whether or not that was a good thing.

CHAPTER
∞~FOUR~∞

MICHELLE SMILED WHEN SHE looked through the peep-hole and recognized her visitor. She opened the door immediately. "Heather? This is a pleasant surprise."

She stood aside as the young girl entered, her smile a replica of her father's. "Hello, Ms. Chapman. Dad gave me your business card and asked that I call you with the information about the number of people attending my party. But when I saw you were only a short walk from school, I decided to drop by instead. I hope you don't mind."

"Of course not. How is school going?"

"Fine. I figured moving to a new town would be hard, meeting a bunch of new friends and all. But everyone here in Lake Falls is nice. I can't imagine living anywhere else now."

Michelle chuckled. "Yes, the town kind of grows on you, doesn't it? By the way, how's your dad?"

"Dad's doing fine. He's busy building webpages for his clients."

"Sounds interesting," Michelle said, leading Heather toward the kitchen.

"It is. I've watched him do it a few times and he seems to enjoy it. One day he's going to show me how it's done."

"You like working with computers?"

"Not as much as Dad, but they're okay."

When they reached the kitchen, Michelle offered Heather a chair at the table. "I was about to fix a snack. Would you like to join me?"

Her guest beamed. "Sure. Do you have any more of those nutty cheese bars? They were delicious."

Michelle laughed. "Yes, I'm sure I have some more around here. They're one of my most popular treats. People call and request them all the time, and I make a batch every day for Lilly's Café.

Michelle studied Heather. The last time she had seen her had been right after her asthma attack, an attack Paul still hadn't acknowledged. In fact, he had quickly left the other day when she had asked him what the doctor had said about Heather's condition. Michelle was quite sure he hadn't taken her to the doctor for a follow-up appointment. Unfortunately, some of the parents she came in contact with through her work with the AANMA didn't believe asthma was a permanent or a dangerous condition. Too late, they discovered it was something they should have taken seriously, and their child should have been on a management plan.

"And how have you been, Heather?" Michelle asked her softly.

"Oh, I've been fine. I'm looking forward to the party. Turning sixteen is going to be super. Jason has already asked Dad if he can take me to the movies the weekend following my birthday."

"Who's Jason?" she asked.

Heather's smile practically told it all. "Jason Sullivan is a guy I know from church and school. He's seventeen and a junior this year. He's supernice."

Michelle chuckled. "I know Jason. His aunt Carrie is a close friend of mine. We went to school together. I know his parents, as well. Connie and Anthony were older and graduated from school before Carrie and me. And you're right, Jason's supernice. The entire Sullivan family is."

"I think Dad likes Jason," Heather said as Michelle placed a plate of goodies along with a glass of milk on the table. "He lets Jason walk me home, but he just can't take me out yet. And on the weekends, he comes over and we watch movies together. Sometimes Dad joins us, but usually he stays in his office to work."

Heather tilted her head as Michelle sat down at the table. "You can come over if you like and watch movies with us, Ms. Chapman. We can make it a foursome. Me and Jason and you and my dad."

Michelle was stunned by the invitation and at first

was speechless. "Thanks," she said at last, "but I'm not sure how your father would feel about that."

Heather waved off her words. "Dad won't mind."

Michelle had to disagree, considering how quickly he'd taken off yesterday.

"These are so good," Heather said, practically licking her lips as she tried a chocolate-studded cookie. "And before I forget the reason I dropped by. I've invited twenty people to my party. Twelve girls and eight boys."

Michelle nodded. "Twenty is a good number, and I already know it's going to be some party."

"I hope so. You only turn sixteen once."

"That's true. I'm going to do everything I can to make it special, and I have just the menu for you. I spoke with Ravine Stokes earlier today and I think you're going to enjoy all the group activities she's come up with. I'll be getting together with your father to present the menu to him, and I'm hoping we'll finalize everything then. Now that I know how many are coming, I can calculate just how much food to prepare."

Heather smiled at her. "Thanks, Ms. Chapman. Dad made a smart move when he hired you. I'm glad he didn't take Ms. Beaumont up on her offer to help."

Michelle pretended not to hear what Heather had said. Ms. Amy had told her that Latisha Beaumont had set her sights on Paul the moment he'd moved to town. Thoughts of the woman being so aggressive should not bother her. After all, Latisha had put out the word a couple of years ago that she was in the market for husband number three. And Paul was definitely a man any woman would be interested in. As Michelle studied Heather's list, she wondered what else Latisha had volunteered to do for Paul, and found it extremely annoying that she even cared.

"I talked to my grandmother last night and told her how well you can bake."

Michelle smiled. "Are your grandparents flying in for the party?"

"No, they're doing missionary work in Africa, but they'll be coming for a visit this summer and we'll celebrate then."

Michelle really liked Heather, and a part of her wanted to ask whether her father had taken her to the doctor, but knowing how Paul felt, she would be out of line to do so. She had asked earlier how Heather was doing and she'd said fine. And she looked fine. But Michelle knew an asthma attack could happen at any moment regardless of how well you looked. And that worried her.

PAUL TOSSED THE PAPERS he'd been reading aside, finding it hard to concentrate. For some reason, Michelle Chapman was on his mind, and had been since she'd dropped by the other day to finalize the menu.

He would have no other contact with her until the party, when she arrived to set things up, and that was a full eight days from now. Why did the thought of not seeing her again until then bother him? He sighed as he leaned back in his chair after staring at his calendar for a moment longer than necessary.

"Hey, Dad."

He glanced up. Heather was standing in the doorway. "Hello, sweetheart. School's out already?"

"Yes. Today is one of those early dismissal days, where we get out at noon. I mentioned it this morning."

She probably had. His mind evidently had been on other things. Or, more specifically, on someone. Sighing deeply, he picked up the document he'd been trying all morning to read.

"I had planned to stop by Ms. Chapman's house on my way home from school," Heather said.

He swung his head up and stared at her. "Why?" He'd known that she had stopped by Michelle's house last week to tell her the number of people coming to her party.

"Because we still have her container—the one she sent those treats in last week. I wanted to get it back to her in case she needed it for another order or something."

He had forgotten all about the container. He could have easily given it to Michelle the other day when she was here. This was the excuse he needed to see her again. "You're right, she might need it. I'll take it over to her now."

"Thanks, Dad."

"No problem."

After Heather left the room, he quickly shut down his computer and moved from behind his desk. A surge of something he hadn't felt in a long time rushed through his veins. There had to be a reason

why he was in such a high-wire mood at the chance
to see Michelle again. There had to be a reason why
he thought of her constantly. And he was determined
to find out what it was. Today.

"COMING!"

Michelle made her way out of her bedroom, entering the hall while putting in an earring. She had
finished all the baking she needed to do that day and
had decided to get out of the house and treat herself
to lunch. Since there weren't too many places where
she could go in Lake Falls if she wanted a meal alone,
she decided to take the drive into Savannah and dine
at one of her favorite restaurants.

She had taken a leisurely bath and slipped on a
sundress she had purchased last month when she
had gone to visit friends in Memphis. She felt good
today. Her Realtor had called that morning and said
the couple leasing her condo were interested in buying it. She had no qualms about selling, which meant
she had made up her mind as to where she wanted
to live permanently. A lot of people would think she
was nuts for giving up the fun and excitement of
Memphis, but she knew what was best for her. Lake
Falls was her home. She hadn't known how much she
missed living here until she had returned.

She glanced out the peephole in her door and
caught her breath. Paul was standing on the other
side. What was he doing here? There was nothing left
for them to discuss. And besides, it still bothered her
that he refused to acknowledge Heather's condition.

A part of her wanted to approach him about it again. But first, she needed to know why he was on her front porch. She inhaled deeply, knowing the only way to find that out was to open the door and ask.

"PAUL, THIS IS A pleasant surprise. I hope everything is all right."

Paul blinked and then for the next couple of seconds just stood there staring, allowing his gaze to roam all over Michelle, starting at the top of her head to the sandals she was wearing. Her hair was pinned up, with a few wispy curls framing her face, the style complimenting her softly rounded features. And then there was her dress, a buttercup-yellow that highlighted her smooth brown skin. She had on very little makeup, which gave her a fresh and wholesome look. A downright sexy look.

"Paul?"

He blinked a second time, realizing she'd said his name again, waiting for him to answer. "No, there's nothing wrong. I'm just returning this."

She glanced down at the container in his hand. "Oh, I'd almost forgotten about it. Come in."

She stepped aside and he entered. "It seems I came at a bad time," he said when she closed the door behind him. "You're about to go out."

She smiled, taking the container from him. "You're fine. I decided to drive to Savannah today and treat myself to lunch. Excuse me while I put this in the kitchen."

He watched her walk off, and wondered what there was about her that attracted him so fiercely. She was a looker, but there was something else, too. It had to be her calm and soothing nature. That had been evident during Heather's reaction to those markers. Or maybe it was because Michelle was one of the few single women in Lake Falls who hadn't deliberately put herself in his path at every opportune moment. If Latisha Beaumont came up with another excuse to call him, he was seriously thinking about having a talk with her. No man liked being harassed, and he was beginning to feel that was exactly what she was doing.

"You really didn't have to come make a special trip to bring that to me," Michelle was saying as she returned to the room. "I have plenty of them."

"No problem. Today is a slow day for me anyway." There was no reason to tell her that he had lots of work to do, but couldn't get in the right frame of mind to do it. "And you're off to Savannah for lunch?"

"Yes, just for a change of pace. I'm going to one of my favorite restaurants."

He nodded. "Are you planning to meet someone there?"

She shook her head and smiled. "No, I'll be dining alone."

Not one to miss an opportunity, Paul asked, "Mind if I join you? I haven't had lunch yet myself, and a good meal in Savannah sounds nice."

He could tell she was surprised by his question,

but her smile didn't waver as she said, "Sure. You can join me if you really want to."

He met her gaze. "I do really want to. We can take my car."

CHAPTER
∽FIVE∽

MICHELLE DIDN'T WANT to think of having lunch with Paul as a date. But what else would you call it when, after leaving Rocco's, they'd strolled hand in hand around Savannah's historic district? It had been a while since she had enjoyed male company, and found that Paul was a likable guy.

She was surprised when he shared a lot about himself, telling her of his parents' missionary work and his eighty-five-year-old grand-aunt Zelda, whom he was very fond of. He didn't say much about his divorce, only that his wife had never wanted kids and could only hang in as a parent for the first five years of Heather's life before splitting. He was quite sure that Heather probably wouldn't know her mother if they were to pass on the street. The disgust in his voice let Michelle know that he was not carrying a torch for his ex.

She also discovered that he was a guy who liked a lot of the same things she did. They enjoyed eating seafood, loved chocolate, preferred watching basketball to football and were members of the same political party. The only thing they differed dramatically on was their taste in movies. She liked watching romantic comedy, whereas he preferred blood, guts and gore.

By the time the scenic walk they had taken was over, it was late afternoon, and he suggested they remain in Savannah for dinner and try out a steak house one of the tour guides had recommended. Once at the restaurant, he called Heather on his cell phone to let her know not to expect him until late. He'd told her where he was, but omitted mentioning that the two of them were together.

When he ended the call, Michelle seized the opportunity to ask him about Heather's health. She could immediately tell from his expression that he didn't appreciate her concern.

She leaned back in her chair. If he thought he had a reason to be irritated with her, then she felt she had a reason to be irritated with him. "Why do you get so uptight whenever I ask about Heather?"

He frowned. "I don't get uptight. I just don't know why you're assuming that something is wrong with my daughter."

Michelle sighed. "I'm not assuming anything, Paul. One asthma attack can be followed by another, which could be dangerous, especially if you don't know the reason for it. I can't help but be concerned. Heather needs to be on an asthma management plan. If you don't feel comfortable taking her to the doctor, at least call the Allergy & Asthma Net—"

"You saw her last week. Did she look ill?" he interrupted tersely.

"No."

"Okay then."

A part of Michelle knew it wasn't okay, but that she would be wasting her time trying to convince him of that. When it came to Heather's asthma, he was determined to keep his head in the sand.

They didn't talk much on the drive back to Lake Falls; the tension between them was as obvious as the reason for it. There were certain aspects of his life that he was determined to keep to himself. She knew he had that right. After all, there was really nothing going on between them. But she had truly enjoyed spending time with him today and couldn't help but be bothered by his attitude.

By the time they arrived back in Lake Falls it was dark. He parked in front of her home and turned off the engine. "I upset you."

She glanced over at him and shook her head. "No, you didn't."

"Yes, I did and I want to apologize."

She met his gaze, expecting him to say more, something that might explain why he was so stubborn when it came to Heather's condition.

"I enjoyed your company," he said, pulling her

thoughts back to the two of them and the fact they were sitting in a parked car in front of her house.

From now on, Michelle decided, she wouldn't bring up anything related to Heather's asthma episode. Even when she couldn't contain her own worry, she would keep it to herself and not share her concern with Paul.

"And I enjoyed your company, as well," she said, and meant it. She refused to let her annoyance with him over Heather ruin what she felt had been a beautiful day.

"How would you like to join me for a cup of coffee and one of my new pastries?" she offered.

He smiled over at her. "I'd love to."

When they began walking together up to the house, he reached out and took her hand in his, just as he'd done most of the day. He released it only when she had to pull her key out of her purse to open the door. He stepped inside behind her and closed the door.

The lights in the entire house were turned off, and when she switched on the lamp next to the sofa, it cast the room in a soft glow. She turned quickly to find Paul standing right in front of her.

"Sorry, I didn't mean to startle you," he said in a husky tone.

"You didn't."

Her insides were quivering, but not because he'd surprised her. It was because he was so close. He had stood next to her several times that day, but for some reason this was different. She probably could blame the soft lighting in the room, which gave it a sort of romantic setting, or possibly the way he was looking at her. His eyes were deep, dark, intense.

"I guess now is a good time to thank you for today," she said. "But I hadn't meant for you to pay for both my meals."

He smiled. "No need to thank me. I enjoyed your company, and I appreciate you letting me tag along."

"You can tag along anytime. I enjoyed your company, as well."

"Mmm, anytime?" he said in a low, husky tone. "I might take you up on your offer."

Michelle parted her lips, but whatever she was about to say was forgotten when he leaned in close, placed his hands around her waist and kissed the words right off her lips. Desire, fueled by need, made her moan when he deepened the kiss. As if sensing her response, he pulled her closer into his arms, molding her soft curves against his hard muscles and stirring a degree of urgency within her that she hadn't felt in a long time. Of their own accord, her arms reached up and wrapped around his neck, and she kissed him back.

Wow! PAUL SLOWLY PULLED his mouth away and leaned back, his arms still wrapped around Michelle's waist. He felt her tremble, and at the same time acknowledged the way his own heart was pounding in his chest. Had passion been bottled up inside of him for so long that, once uncapped, it had unleashed emotions he'd forgotten he could feel? Emotions that were now eating away at him, making him long for something he'd thought he could do without.

He watched as Michelle raised her hand and touched the lips that he'd just kissed. "I don't know if that was a good idea," she said softly.

He leaned closer, coming within mere inches of her mouth, and breathed, "That, Michelle, was the best idea I've had in a long time."

Then he kissed her again, glorying in her automatic response and not allowing either of them to deny what they were feeling. Skyrocketing passion. An overload of desire. He had wanted to seduce her with his mouth, but found she was seducing him with hers instead.

He pulled back slowly, reluctantly, but knowing that he had to. One part of his mind screamed that they were moving too fast. But another taunted they weren't moving fast enough. The attraction had been there from the first and they were finally acting on it.

"I think I'd better go," he said softly, taking a step back and releasing his hands from around her waist.

"But what about your treat?"

He smiled. "I just enjoyed it, and it was well worth the wait."

LATER THAT NIGHT, after Michelle had gotten into bed, she took the time to reflect on just how her day with Paul had gone.

He had said that he would see her tomorrow, and she believed him. She just wasn't sure where all this would lead. A few days ago she hadn't been the least bit interested in becoming involved with a man, but being around Paul today had reminded her what it was like to share a special relationship with someone.

But then, she couldn't forget that Paul was deliberately keeping her at bay when it came to Heather's health. Each time she brought up the subject, he closed her out.

She cuddled under the covers, not wanting to think about the time and energy she'd devoted to her last relationship with a man. All the hours she had spent trying to make Lonnie happy, to make him appreciate her. Did she really want to go through that again? Especially now, when growing her business should be her top priority?

But then all she had to do was remember how much she had enjoyed herself today, how special being with Paul had been. A part of her was convinced that having Paul Castlewood in her life wouldn't be all bad.

THE NEXT MORNING Paul found Heather in the kitchen, sitting at the table, eating breakfast before school. She'd been in bed by the time he'd gotten home the previous night. She glanced over at him now and smiled. "Hi, Dad. Did you enjoy yourself in Savannah yesterday?"

He crossed the room, heading straight for the coffeepot. "What makes you think I was in Savannah having fun?" He'd made absolutely certain not to mention anything on the phone about Michelle being with him.

"Come on, Dad, I know that you and Ms. Chapman were together. By now I'm sure the entire town knows."

He frowned. "What do you mean, the entire town?"

"Eli Sessions's mom saw the two of you while she was in Savannah, shopping. She couldn't wait to get back to town and tell Lois Dunlap."

"I see," he said, sitting down at the table with his cup of coffee. And he did see. It was called small-town gossip.

"I think it's cool."

He smiled as he took a sip of coffee. "You would. But don't get your hopes up. There was nothing much to it. We just had lunch together."

"And dinner."

Paul grinned. "Okay, we had lunch *and* dinner." He checked the clock on the stove. "Shouldn't you be leaving for school about now?"

Heather smiled. "Yes. I will in a moment. I just want to know one thing."

He lifted a brow. "What?"

"Will you take her out again? Are the two of you an item?"

"You said you wanted to know just one thing," Paul teased. "Choose which one."

"Okay. Are the two of you an item?"

"Depends on what you mean by 'an item.'"

"Dad!"

He set his coffee cup down. "All right. All right.

To answer your question, the answer is maybe. That was our first date."

"So you would call it a date?"

"That's what I'd call it, but I'm sure your generation probably has another name for it."

Heather rolled her eyes. "It's still called dating, Dad."

"I'm glad to hear that." He stared at his daughter for a long moment. "So what do you think?"

"About you seeing Ms. Chapman?"

"Yes."

A huge grin covered Heather's face. "I told you what I thought. I like her. I think it's cool."

He grinned back, thinking just how much he loved his kid. "Yes, I think it's cool, too."

MICHELLE HUNG UP the phone. If another person called to congratulate her on reeling in Paul, she was going to scream. She'd all but snapped at Lori Coffee, telling her in no uncertain terms that Paul Castlewood was not a fish, he was a man. Men didn't get reeled in. She sighed in disgust. That was the one thing she could do without in a small town—everyone wanting to know your business. She and Paul had shared lunch and dinner, not made plans for a lifetime commitment. Why did everyone assume they had?

The phone rang again and Michelle was about to ignore it when she glanced at the caller ID. It was her friend Brittany Howard, who worked at the headquarters of AANMA. They'd met in college, and Brittany was the person who'd been instrumental in bringing Michelle on board as a volunteer outreach service coordinator. Both she and Brittany suffered from asthma. Giving each other support during their college days had made the condition a lot easier to cope with.

What Michelle enjoyed the most about her volunteer work was the part she played in giving the public a greater understanding of asthma. AANMA was growing by leaps and bounds, spreading the word through a number of national events and other outreach programs.

She quickly picked up the phone. "Britt? How are you?"

"Fine. I'm just calling to make sure you got enough supplies for the school nurses."

Brittany's question made Michelle recall the incident with Heather. Paul still hadn't acknowledged that she had had an asthma attack.

"Plenty, thanks," Michelle told Brittany.

They talked for a few minutes, and Michelle had just hung up when she heard a loud knock at her door. From where she was standing she couldn't tell who was there, but she could see the car parked in front.

Paul.

She thought of the number of calls she'd received that morning and figured he'd gotten wind that the whole town was talking about them. Was he upset? Was that the reason he was at her house before ten o'clock in the morning?

Michelle sighed as she headed toward the door. There was only one way to find out.

CHAPTER
SIX

DURING THE DRIVE over to Michelle's house, Paul kept asking himself what he was doing. Why on earth would he want to become seriously involved with a woman after all these years? A woman he'd known less than a month.

The answer was blatantly obvious the moment she opened the door. He experienced a storm of emotions that only she could stir up inside of him. Was she worth all the craziness of waking up in the wee hours of the night just to recall a smile that he couldn't forget?

Yes, she was worth it.

He sighed deeply, and when she gave him the smile that had been his downfall from the first, he couldn't help but return it. "Good morning. I hate bothering you so early, but we need to talk." Paul knew what he had to do, what he had to say.

Michelle nodded and stepped aside, closing the door behind him when he entered. "I know why you're here," she said.

He placed his hands in the pockets of his jeans. "Do you?"

"Yes." She moved away from the door to stand in front of him. "My phone hasn't stopped ringing all morning, and I apologize for that."

He lifted a brow. Evidently there was something he was missing. "Your phone has been ringing all morning and you want to apologize to *me* for it?"

"Yes."

"You want to tell me why?"

She went over to the sofa and sat down. "Someone has spread a rumor that the two of us are seeing each other."

"And?"

She frowned. "And that's not true."

He moved to sit in the chair across from her. "We did spend the better part of yesterday together in Savannah."

"Yes, but it wasn't what everyone assumes."

"Maybe not. However, we did share a kiss."

He could see the blush that appeared on her face. "I know but—"

He held up his hand, stopping what she was about to say. "Does it bother you that people are thinking that way about us?"

She shrugged. "No, but this is a small town and people will quickly assume what you might not want them to assume. I'm catering your daughter's birthday party, which means we're involved in a business relationship. I don't want to jeopardize that. And I'm beginning to think of you as more than a friend and don't want to jeopardize that, either."

He took a deep breath. She still wasn't getting the point he was trying to make. He eased out of his chair and walked over to where she was sitting. "Scoot over for a second."

He saw the surprised look on her face, but she did as he asked, and he sat down beside her. "Now, then, let me explain something to you." He smiled, and for the first time in a long time felt he was doing something right.

"I like you," he said bluntly, taking her hand in his. He remembered walking around and holding hands with her yesterday. It had seemed like the most natural thing to do. "I mean, I genuinely like you, Michelle, and I'd like to get to know you better. I propose that we become involved."

She blinked. "Involved?"

"Yes, involved. You know, you, me, doing things together like we did yesterday. Sharing lunch and dinner, an occasional movie, walking in the park, holding hands." He raised their joined hands. "I like holding hands with you."

He leaned back against the sofa and studied her expression. "So what do you think about that?"

MICHELLE REALLY DIDN'T KNOW what to think about it. She would be the first to admit that she had enjoyed their time together yesterday. And hadn't she reached the conclusion that he was a very likable guy? When he'd brought her home last night and kissed her, it was a kiss destined to become embedded in her brain cells forever. And hadn't she decided that having Paul in her life wasn't such a bad idea?

Or *was* it? There was still one thing that bothered her, namely his willful blindness to Heather's condition.

But should Michelle let that one thing stand in the way? If she kept working on him to acknowledge his daughter's asthma, would he eventually come around, or continue to close her out? He wanted them to become involved, so at least that was a start, but still, she refused to rush into anything. He had pretty much defined just what "involved" meant to him, and it all sounded great, but she couldn't help remembering Lonnie and all the time and effort she'd put into making things between them work only to find out she'd wanted more out of their relationship than he had.

She gently pulled her hand from Paul's and rose to her feet. She stared down at him. "It's been a while since I've been involved with anyone. Maybe I tend to expect more out of relationships than I should." She might as well be honest. "The last guy I dated, I ended up living with for a while when I thought things between us were pretty tight. Then he got a promotion at work that made it imperative for him to move to another state. But he didn't think I was important enough to move with him." She paused for a moment and then added, "I came home from work one day and he was packing."

She saw Paul's jaw stiffen and knew he was angry on her behalf even before he said anything. "It was his loss. Any man who would walk away and leave you behind can't have been in his right mind."

His words touched her in a way that was hard to explain. All she knew was that she suddenly wanted to be held by him, so she eased back down beside him.

As if he knew what she needed, he pulled her into his arms and kissed her. It seemed he was trying to wipe away her hurt, and she appreciated the effort.

When he ended the kiss, he still held her close. "So do we become involved, Michelle?" he asked in a deep, husky tone.

She looked up at him. "Yes, but do you have any objections to holding off until after Heather's party?"

"No," he said quietly. "I don't have any objections as long as there's a good reason you want us to."

She shrugged. "This is a small town and I want to stay focused on giving Heather the best birthday party possible. I want the attention to be on her next week, and not on us. We owe her that."

Paul threw his head back and laughed. "No wonder Heather likes you so much."

Michelle lifted an eyebrow. "She does?"

"I told you that."

She nodded. "You said she liked me—but a lot?"

"She likes you a whole lot. Now, I'll go along with

what you want. We'll wait until after Heather's party, but then we begin acting like a normal couple."

Michelle wasn't sure such a thing was possible in Lake Falls, especially when he was considered such a hot prospect. But before she could say anything else, Paul was kissing her again.

CHAPTER
∽SEVEN∽

"NICE PARTY. And these are for you, by the way." Michelle smiled up at Paul before accepting the beautiful bouquet of fresh flowers. She lowered her head to inhale their fragrance. They smelled simply divine. "Thank you. What are they for?"

"This." He indicated the room. "Like I said, it's a nice party and it wouldn't have happened without you."

Although she felt he was giving her far more credit than she rightly deserved, she knew what he meant. Ravine Stokes, the party planner, had come down with the flu a few days before the event and Michelle had stepped in to take her place.

"Thanks," she said, following his gaze around the room. The main thing was that Heather was pleased with her party.

"Well, it's almost over. Now we can concentrate on other things."

Paul's words made her shiver. There was no way to stop the anticipation flowing through her.

"Do you think everyone is enjoying the food?" she asked as a way of changing the subject. His grin indicated he had caught on.

"I don't know why they wouldn't be, since you did an outstanding job. If Brian Frazier eats another one of those lemon squares, he's going to leave here with puckered lips."

Michelle grinned. Paul was right. The teen had gobbled up a number of the treats already.

"I have to make a drive to Brunswick on Thursday. Do you want to come along for the ride?"

She looked at him. "Brunswick?"

"Yes. I'm meeting with a potential client there. I thought that afterward you and I could do lunch."

What he proposed sounded like fun. "Okay. I'd like that."

He checked his watch. "Time to make our rounds. That Summers girl is missing again."

Michelle nodded and walked beside him as he moved around the room. Earlier, the two of them had watched as Rachel Summers had tried coaxing Brad Parker to go outside with her.

When Rachel was nowhere to be found, Michelle followed Paul into the kitchen and stepped outside— just in time to interrupt a kiss.

"The party is inside," Paul said, startling the two teens.

Rachel, who was only fifteen but acted older, smiled over at them. "You're right, but we thought we would get some fresh air."

Paul didn't smile back. "Not tonight. I guess you'll just have to settle for the stuffy air inside until your mother comes for you."

Brad didn't say anything, but nodded before following Rachel back inside.

"The Summerses need to keep a closer eye on that girl," Paul said when the pair was no longer within hearing range.

"I agree." Michelle had been around Paul and Heather enough that week to know he took parenting seriously. Although it was obvious Heather had a crush on Jason, she always behaved in a respectful way.

The remainder of the party went well, and by midnight, all the kids had left and the food had been eaten. Heather offered to help with the cleanup but Paul and Michelle convinced her they could handle things and that she should go on to bed and rest after such a busy day.

"You're lucky, you know," Michelle said to Paul while they were taking down the streamers and balloons. "Heather is such a wonderful girl, and I'm not just saying that because she's your daughter. Rachel Summers could learn a few things from her."

Paul nodded. "I hope you're right."

Michelle hoped that she was right, as well. Having a friend like Rachel had to be a challenge for Heather. Although Rachel had been with Brad outside, Michelle had noticed the girl making a play at one time or another for all the guys at the party. "Would you and Heather like to come over for dinner tomorrow?"

Paul couldn't help but smile as he pulled Michelle into his arms. "Is that going to be our official way of announcing to everyone that we're involved?"

She tilted up her head and smiled back at him. "Yes, I think that would be a perfect way."

It was close to two o'clock in the morning when Michelle arrived home. Paul had insisted on following behind her to make sure she got there safely. She had waved him goodbye and then on impulse had blown him a kiss before going inside. She was tired, but in a good way, and was glad the party had been such a huge success.

Before getting into bed, Michelle glanced over at her flowers. They were beautiful and filled her bedroom with their fragrance. The bouquet had been a nice gesture on Paul's part and she appreciated his thoughtfulness. Over the past week she'd discovered that she and Paul were so at ease with each other. She'd been busy putting the final touches on the party and he had been busy meeting a deadline for one of his clients' websites. But they had managed to talk on the phone late at night, when most of Lake Falls was asleep.

And now they had decided to make everything public.

As she got into bed and snuggled under the covers, she was again reminded of the kisses they had shared. She had enjoyed each and every one of them. She had made a number of mistakes with Lonnie, mistakes she didn't intend to repeat. But she had a feeling that Paul was genuine in his affection and would never do anything to lead her on. Now that the party was over they could turn up the heat a bit, and she could hardly wait.

CHAPTER
~EIGHT~

A WEEK LATER, as Michelle sat across the table from Paul, she couldn't help but reflect on the amount of time they'd spent together. He had joined her for dinner on Sunday with Heather. On Tuesday night, Paul and Michelle had gone to the movies. They'd had breakfast together on Wednesday morning, shared dinner in Brunswick on Thursday and here it was Saturday and they were dining together again. This was their first public dinner date in Lake Falls.

"How is your meat?"

Her smile widened. "Wonderful. They may be a mom-and-pop operation, but Wilson's Steakhouse serves the best steaks on the East Coast."

Paul chuckled. "I have to agree." He leaned back in his chair. "So do you have a busy week ahead?"

She met his gaze. "No more than usual. The Foy-

ers are celebrating their fiftieth wedding anniver-
sary and I'm meeting with their daughter to plan a
menu. The guest list, I understand, will be well over
a hundred people."

"That's a lot of food."

"Yes, but I'm going to enjoy doing it." She took a
sip of her iced tea. "And by the way, I'm having several young people over next Saturday. All of them
have had an asthma attack at some point. As part of
AANMA's awareness drive, we're having a guest
speaker who is going to show us how to use a peak
flow meter and holding chamber and discuss the ben-
efits of a written asthma management plan."

He lifted a brow. "And?"

"And I wanted your permission to invite Heather."

She could tell by his expression that he had a problem giving it. His next words confirmed her obser-
vation. "We've been over this before, Michelle, and I
don't understand why you feel Heather needs a management plan. What happened to her a few weeks
ago—"

"Could happen again, Paul," she interjected. "Why
is it so hard for you to understand that, or better yet,
why are you refusing to do so?"

He frowned. "Mainly because I don't think Heather's condition is as serious as you tend to make it."

Michelle sighed. And that was the problem. Most
people underestimated the seriousness of asthma
symptoms until it was too late. "A few weeks ago,
you said you wanted us to build a relationship, yet

even now you refuse to take seriously something that I know and feel very strongly about."

"It's not that I don't take it seriously. It's just I don't think it applies to Heather. Do you really think I'd jeopardize my daughter's health?"

"No, I don't think that, Paul."

"Then what, exactly, do you think?"

They were doing nothing but going around in circles, as far as she was concerned. "Let's just drop it."

She felt him closing her out again. How could they pursue a serious relationship when he constantly did that?

She was not surprised when he refused her invitation to join her for coffee and a snack at her place, saying he had a big project to work on. She knew he was intentionally putting distance between them.

That was fine; she would deal with it…or maybe she wouldn't. She had hoped his attitude would change once they began seeing each other, but it hadn't.

There was more to building a relationship than the occasional dinner together, some heated kisses. There was also that shared sense of connection, the feeling that your thoughts and deepest convictions were taken seriously. And that was what disturbed her the most, knowing that even after all this time, she and Paul were no closer to resolving their differences about Heather's condition than they had been before.

Ms. AMY WAS staring at her.

"What is it?" Michelle asked.

"You look rather sad," the older woman said with concern in her eyes.

Michelle drew in a deep breath and then slowly exhaled. Ms. Amy had dropped by for lunch and they were sitting in the kitchen, eating chicken-salad sandwiches and enjoying cold glasses of lemonade. They had been talking about the weather, when Michelle's mind had wandered and she'd begun thinking about Paul. The last time she had seen him was almost a week ago. He had called once or twice to say he was tied up with a major client, but part of her felt he was deliberately putting distance between them.

"Do I?" she asked now, deciding not to pretend for the older woman. It wouldn't do any good anyway. She was sure Ms. Amy was fully aware things had cooled between them.

"Do you want to talk about it, Michelle?"

Michelle took another sip of her lemonade, knowing it wouldn't help to talk about it. Things were as they were, and wishing wouldn't change that.

Suddenly, an emotion she thought she would never feel again ripped through her, making her tremble so much that she had to place the glass she was holding on the table.

"Michelle? Are you okay?"

She glanced over at Ms. Amy and swallowed. How could she explain that she'd just realized she had fallen in love with Paul?

She was spared from having to explain anything when her phone rang. "Excuse me." She got up from the table to answer it.

She recognized Paul's voice immediately, and another shiver ran up her spine. Regardless of how things were between them, she missed him. But the pleasure she'd felt at hearing his voice suddenly died. "When?" she asked as she tried to calm her racing heart.

At his response, she nodded. "All right, I'm on my way."

She quickly hung up and glanced over at Ms. Amy. "That was Paul. He was calling from the hospital. Heather was taken there from school after suffering another asthma attack."

MICHELLE ARRIVED AT THE hospital and went straight to the E.R. Paul was sitting in the waiting room but rushed over when he saw her. He pulled her into his arms and clung to her tightly.

When he drew back moments later, she saw the haggard look on his face. "I should have listened to you," he said brokenly. "How many times did you suggest that I check into Heather's condition? I should have taken her to the doctor! Then this wouldn't have happened. She's on a ventilator now and I can't even see her."

Michelle led him back to the chair. "What did the doctor say?"

"She had another asthma attack. I spoke with the school principal and *she* said she knew it was an asthma attack because of the in-service class you taught a few weeks ago. She followed the instructions in the materials supplied by your organization. Otherwise they don't know what they would have done."

He sighed deeply and then said in a shaken voice, "Twice now you've saved my daughter's life, and I want to thank you and that organization you volunteer for."

Michelle didn't say anything as Paul continued to grip her hand. She could imagine what he was going through. By the time she'd reached her sixteenth birthday she had been hospitalized for the condition at least five times. That was one of the reasons she volunteered for AANMA. There were so many people who assumed that asthma was a way of life and had no idea it was also a way of death if not treated properly.

"I should have taken her to the doctor," Paul said again.

Michelle knew she didn't have to tell him he should have. He wasn't the first and, unfortunately, he wouldn't be the last who would make that mistake. The important thing now was for Heather to get better.

"Have you seen her at all?" she asked him.

"I saw her briefly when I first got here. She was gasping for breath, could barely breathe. The doctor asked me to step out while they connected her to a ventilator. That was over an hour ago. What's happening to her? What is the asthma doing to her?"

That, at least, was something Michelle could explain. "When asthma occurs, usually three things happen. The lining of the airway swells. Cells overproduce mucus, which starts clogging the passage-ways, and the surrounding muscles tighten."

"What do you think brought it on?" he asked.

She inhaled deeply. "It could have been caused by a number of things. The doctor should be able to give you more specifics when you talk to him."

Paul glanced around nervously. "Why is it taking so long? When will they give me an update about how she's doing?"

Michelle understood his frustration. "I'm sure they will soon. For now let's just give them time to do what's needed."

Paul nodded and squeezed her hand again. "Thanks for being here with me, Michelle."

"Under the circumstances, I wouldn't want to be anywhere else."

And she meant it. Paul and Heather had become part of her life. She looked forward to Heather's after-school visits, and when the teen had mentioned she would love to learn how to bake, they had discussed the possibility of Michelle starting a cooking class on Saturday mornings for some of the young women in the community.

"Mr. Castlewood?" It was Heather's doctor, Paul quickly told her.

Paul quickly got to his feet, pulling Michelle with him. "How is she?" he asked, sounding on the verge of panic.

"Heather will be okay. We've sedated her and she's resting comfortably now. We're not sure what brought on this attack but we're doing a series of tests to pinpoint the cause."

"I thought she had outgrown her asthma," Paul said, sounding defeated.

The doctor nodded in understanding. "A lot of parents think that, especially if an attack hasn't taken place in a while. Asthma attacks can be separated by years. That doesn't mean the condition is gone. You and Heather are new to this area. The attacks could be caused by her body getting used to the air she's now breathing. There are a number of paper mills down the road in Brunswick."

"I'll do whatever I have to. Even move away if that will make my daughter better."

"I don't think you have to go that far," the doctor said wryly. "We just need to establish Heather on a solid asthma management plan. Pretty soon she'll be leaving for college. You'll want her to be able to live a fulfilling life anywhere in the country she wants to go, not someplace that's dictated by her condition."

Paul nodded. "When can I see my daughter?"

"You can see her now, but you need to know what to expect. She's sedated, of course, and on a ventilator to help her breathe, and there are a lot of tubes connecting her to the machine. If her condition continues to improve, we'll be able to remove the ventilator so she can breathe on her own by tomorrow."

Moments later, walking hand in hand, Paul and Michelle followed a nurse through the E.R. doors to the intensive care unit. Michelle felt Paul's fingers tighten on hers the moment he saw his daughter, and standing so close to him, she could feel his body tremble.

"Remember what the doctor said, Paul. Heather is going to be okay."

Instead of answering, he pulled her into his arms, as if he needed whatever strength she had to pass on to him.

"I let my little girl down," he said moments later when he released her and glanced over at the bed.

"No, you didn't," Michelle said softly. "You didn't fully know or understand her condition. But you do now, and organizations like AANMA can help out. The important thing is for us to get Heather well and to keep her that way."

Paul lifted Michelle's hand up to his lips and kissed her knuckles. "Us," he said softly, meeting her gaze.

She smiled, not wanting to read more into the word, not exactly certain what he was implying. But for the moment, she wanted to reassure him. "Yes. Us."

NOT WANTING TO LEAVE Heather alone, they both remained at the hospital for the rest of the day. In the wee hours of the night, they rotated watch duty so each of them could go home to shower and change clothes.

Jason visited the next morning, and Michelle could tell how shaken up he was about what had happened to Heather. She was appreciative when Paul took Jason downstairs to talk to him, to reassure the young man that Heather would be okay. She knew Paul's respect and admiration for Jason had gone up another notch.

The doctors decided that, since Heather was breathing comfortably on her own, they would remove the ventilator. However, it would be a few hours before the sedation wore off and she opened her eyes to acknowledge their presence.

Michelle and Paul were in the room when she came to, and she smiled at them before quickly dozing off again. Paul, overjoyed at seeing that his daughter was doing a lot better, pulled Michelle into his arms and kissed her, letting her feel all the happiness that was a part of him at that very moment.

"Wow! I liked that," Michelle said, smiling up at him when he ended the kiss.

He chuckled. "Glad to hear it, because I happen to like you."

A few moments later, when a nurse came in to take Heather's vital signs, they decided to go downstairs to the coffee shop. They were about to get on the elevator when Rachel Summers stepped off.

"Hey, Rachel." When Michelle saw the stricken look on the young girl's face, she quickly asked, "Are you okay?"

"I wanted to see how Heather is doing. I wasn't at school yesterday, and when I got there today, everyone was saying she was in a bad way and they had to call an ambulance."

"Yes, but she's doing better now," Paul said reassuringly.

"Do you think I can see her? Heather has been a good friend to me." Rachel wiped away her tears.

"Well, I'm sure she'd be glad to see you," Michelle said, placing a comforting hand on her shoulder. "But you'll have to check with the nurse. I think visitors are limited in Intensive Care."

Rachel's features brightened. "I'll go find out. Thanks."

Paul and Michelle watched as the girl quickly walked away, and then Paul punched the elevator button again. "Do you know what I think?" he asked Michelle when Rachel was no longer in sight.

"No, what do you think?"

"I think that somehow Heather has been a positive influence in Rachel's life."

Michelle smiled. "Yes, I think you're right."

"I HOPE I NEVER have to go through anything like that again," Heather was saying as she sat up in bed in her hospital room. Paul and Michelle had returned to find that Rachel was there and Jason had returned. Heather was anxiously awaiting her first meal in over twenty-four hours.

"Michelle and I are going to make sure you don't," Paul said, pulling Michelle to his side and placing his arm around her shoulders. "There's this asthma network that Michelle is affiliated with, and they're going to help us set up an asthma management plan for you. We spoke with your doctor earlier and he will be working with the team on it."

"Cool. And do you know what would be even cooler, Dad?"

"No, what?"

"If you and Ms. Chapman could get a little serious."

Paul looked confused. "About what?"

"Each other."

He couldn't help but laugh out loud at his daughter's candidness. "Michelle and I *are* serious about each other. We're just taking things one day at a time and getting to know each other better. When we think the time is right to make any kind of commitment, you'll be the first to know."

"Promise?"

Paul took Michelle's hand in his and held it up for his daughter to see. He smiled at Michelle before turning back to Heather. "Yes, we promise. But the most important thing is for you to get well so we can get out of here and back home."

HEATHER, DRIVEN BY the belief that her father's happiness hinged on her good health, worked hard at recovering. On the fourth day she was overjoyed that the doctor released her from the hospital. Once back home, she was her old self again.

"Not so fast, young lady," Paul had to say when she immediately wanted to get on the phone to call all of her friends. "The first thing you're going to do is subscribe to that *Allergy and Asthma Today* magazine. I borrowed a copy from Michelle and it's very informative reading."

Heather rolled her eyes. "I'm taking your word for it, Dad."

Later that day, Paul went over to Michelle's place. She was busy taking a batch of chocolate-chip squares out of the oven, and invited Paul to eat a couple with a glass of milk.

"Thanks," he said, sliding into a chair at the table. "But first…" Reaching out, he snagged her elbow and pulled her down into his lap.

She grinned at him. "Is there a reason you're keeping me from my work?"

He smiled. "Yes. This."

And then he captured her mouth with his, kissing her thoroughly. She moaned, aware of the intense desire that consumed them both. When Paul finally ended the kiss, he pressed his forehead against hers and sighed deeply.

His heart was pounding rapidly in his chest and he knew now was the time. She had been there for him. And for Heather. He enjoyed her company, but most importantly, he loved her. This strong emotion he was feeling, that he had been feeling for quite a while, just had to be love.

"I need to explain something to you."

She looked at him. "What?"

"The reason I didn't want to accept that Heather hadn't outgrown her asthma."

"Okay, what's the reason?"

"Emma, my ex-wife. She never wanted children, and Heather was not planned…. She never let me forget it. She tried convincing me that we weren't ready for a baby and she should get an abortion. I was totally against it. The day Heather was born, Emma looked at her and had the nerve to say that she would be nothing but trouble for us. And each time Heather got sick for any reason, I always got an 'I told you so' glare from her mom. It wasn't that Heather was a sickly child. She had the normal childhood illnesses, but Emma would use any reason to try and make her point. And after our daughter's first asthma attack, Emma left. She walked out of my life and Heather's."

He sighed. "I've been protective of Heather since then, probably overprotective. And when you kept bringing up the possibility that she had this condition that could come back, instead of taking your warning in a positive way, I took it as a negative."

Michelle nodded as understanding dawned. "The last thing you needed was another woman dwelling on the issue of your daughter's health."

"Yes. And that's why I always went on the defensive about it. I was wrong in doing that and I apologize. You have been the best thing to come into our lives. We love you. I love you."

He took her hand in his. "Marry me," he whispered, feeling the words coming straight from his heart. "If you want we can have a long engagement, but I want to know you are promised to me and one day our futures will be entwined. Will you marry me?"

Tears clouded Michelle's eyes. She didn't need any additional time to think about it. When Paul had told her about his ex and that she hadn't loved the child they had made together, Michelle's heart had gone out to both Paul and Heather. She knew that she was willing to step in and be the woman they needed in their lives, and to love them unconditionally.

"Yes, I'll marry you," she said, her voice quavering with all the emotions she felt. "And it doesn't matter what the state of Heather's health is. I will always love her. I promise."

And then she leaned in and gave him a kiss that sealed their love and the promise she had just made. He was everything she could want in a man, and Heather was all that she wanted in a daughter. Her life was filled with more happiness than she thought possible. And she was ready to move toward the next stage of her life. With Paul.

"DADDY, PLEASE TELL ME a story." Paul smiled as his three-year-old daughter crawled onto his lap. He glanced out the window to see his parents and Michelle busy decorating the yard for Heather's coming-home party. It was hard to believe his oldest daughter had completed college at the University of Georgia, earning a degree in business, and was coming home for the summer to help Michelle with her catering business before taking a job in the fall with a corporation in Boston.

"Daddy?"

He glanced down at the bundle of joy in his lap. "Yes, Amy?"

"A story."

He chuckled. Amy had been born two years after their wedding. Life was better than good. He had two beautiful daughters and a wife he loved more each day.

Heather hadn't had another asthma attack, but remained on a management plan. Like Michelle, she was now an outreach service coordinator with AANMA.

"What story do you want to hear?" he asked his daughter, who'd been named after Ms. Amy Poole, the town matriarch, who'd been instrumental in getting him and Michelle together.

"The one about the three bears."

Paul smiled. "All right."

He was about to begin his narration when he looked up to see Michelle walk in. "I thought I'd come inside and check on you two," she said, leaning down and placing a kiss on his lips.

"We're fine. Amy wants to hear the story about the three bears."

Michelle grinned and said in a low voice, "No need. Look."

Paul followed Michelle's gaze to see Amy had fallen asleep in his arms. "Oh, well."

Michelle smiled. "Yes, oh, well."

Once they'd tucked Amy into bed, they stood in the doorway of her room and smiled at the sight of her sleeping peacefully. Michelle turned to her husband. "Life has been good."

Paul nodded as he drew her closer. His mouth curved into a smile. "Yes, it has. Thanks for loving me."

She leaned closer. "It has been my pleasure." And she stood on tiptoe, captured his mouth with hers and demonstrated to him just how much.

* * * * *

Dear Reader,

I was honored to be asked to be one of the contributing authors for this year's *More Than Words* edition.

From the moment I was introduced to Allergy & Asthma Network Mothers of Asthmatics (AANMA), I was inspired to write a very special love story. And talking to Nancy Sander, the organization's founder, was like putting the icing on the cake. I learned so much information and gained valuable insight as to the severity of asthma, as well as the support AANMA provides.

Then, in the midst of writing this story, I encountered my own near tragedy when my cousin was rushed to the emergency room, where he spent the next five days fighting for his life after having a severe asthma attack. I was able to share what I'd learned from my research about asthma with family members and friends. And I saw firsthand the importance of having an organization like AANMA.

Paul and Michelle's story is a very special one and I hope it moves you to help raise awareness and much-needed funds for organizations as admirable as this one. Please visit www.aanma.org to learn more about AANMA.

Happy reading!
Brenda Jackson

JOAN CLAYTON &
INA ANDRE

⌁—Windfall Basics—⌁

There's something about stepping into a brand-new skirt or throwing on a new jacket that makes a person feel like a million dollars. Yet for many of those struck by poverty and hardship, new clothing, and the upbeat feeling that accompanies it, is a luxury they're unlikely to enjoy.

In 1991 Joan Clayton and Ina Andre, two friends from Toronto, Ontario, decided to change that after walking through a local store one day and asking themselves a simple question: What happens to all the stylish clothing that doesn't sell?

After conducting some research, they arrived at the heartbreaking answer. Many of the brand-new garments ended up in a Dumpster, eventually making their way to a landfill site.

"If there's surplus out there that nobody wants, you might as well put it to good use," says Joan today.

The concept was really that simple. Ask clothing manufacturers and retailers to donate clothes they didn't want or couldn't sell, and Ina and Joan would distribute them to people who could use them.

Fortunately, it was a tried-and-true concept that had already put their first nonprofit on the map. Six years before, in 1985, Ina and Joan launched Second Harvest to address the growing problem of hunger in Toronto. They took perfectly edible food from restaurants and small grocery stores, which would otherwise be going to waste, and reclaimed it to provide thousands of tasty meals to a number of social services across the city.

At first the clothing venture was small, merely a tangential component of their work at Second Harvest. Ina and Joan drove the clothing around in a station wagon and used their dining rooms as storage space. But while making a dropoff at a shelter for homeless men, they heard a staff member remark, "If you give a man clean underwear, he'll go take a shower." The comment struck home and galvanized Ina and Joan to secure start-up funding, gain support from the city's mayor and the media, and incorporate their new charitable organization as Windfall Clothing Service—all in less than two months.

Soon, fashion heavyweights from Levi Strauss & Co. Canada to Gap Inc. started to give new clothes and funding to Windfall. At one point, two tractor-trailers jam-packed with the previous season's athletic shoes showed up ready to unload.

"We found out really early in the game that running shoes get thrown out in the garbage because their style changes so rapidly," says Joan.

"It was incredible. Just amazing," agrees Ina.

The organization's growth has been just as astounding. Employing a small but supremely dedicated staff, this past year Windfall ran like a well-oiled sewing machine and processed over nine hundred thousand pieces of clothing, valued at more than twenty-eight million dollars retail. A local trucking distribution company donates shipping, so clothing can shoot around the city and into the hands of the people who need it within forty-eight hours. The timing makes it easier for one hundred social service agencies to distribute the clothing to those caught in the cycle of poverty. Between Second Harvest and Windfall, Joan and Ina's work and vision, not to mention thousands of hours of volunteer time, have touched the lives of over one million people in Toronto.

"When we had our two hatchback cars and the dining-room table, did we ever think this would be the kind of operation it is now? Of course not," says Ina.

They have much to be proud of—and much to lament.

"I'm amazed that the need is still so terribly strong. The level of poverty in this very wealthy city has deepened. The people at Second Harvest and Windfall are able to make just a tiny dent," she explains.

The fact that Windfall gives out new clothes is

important, Joan and Ina know. The growing numbers of people living in poverty are used to receiving others' castoffs and hand-me-downs, but a new item of clothing is difficult to come by.

"But for women going out for a job interview who have never really had anything new and stylish, it's very special," Ina declares. "It really boosts self-esteem."

It also means people who thought they couldn't even afford to go to job interviews are now agreeing to meet employers in person—and, wearing new clothes to school themselves, their children get an ego boost, too. In fact, Windfall is always searching for new children's clothes and accessories to deal with the swelling number of financially deprived kids who simply want a pair of jeans that fit, a winter jacket that looks new, or a backpack to carry books and their homework in.

Joan and Ina, now in their late seventies, generally stay at arm's length from day-to-day activities, but say they're amazed by the expertise and enthusiasm of Helen Harakas, their executive director, who recently added Windfall's KIDPACKS to their Clothes for Kids program. With the help of volunteers and media, last year Windfall distributed twelve hundred backpacks filled with school supplies, so fewer children would have to carry schoolbooks home in plastic bags.

"This way they're like all the other kids," states Ina, who lets slip that Joan was elbow-deep in pencils and rulers the day they stuffed the bags.

Joan *does* seem to have endless supplies of energy. She moved heavy boxes around warehouse floors into her sixties, and today volunteers with the Labyrinth Community Network, which created and maintains one of the first labyrinths in a Canadian public park in downtown Toronto. Anyone can use a labyrinth for reflection and meditation. In 2004 Joan was awarded the Order of Canada and an honorary Doctor of Civil Law from the University of King's College in Halifax, Nova Scotia.

As for Ina, she recently retired as a student liaison at a theater school and is going to continue her work with Second Harvest in a public relations capacity. She is also hunting for another charity that speaks to her need to help people and add dignity, grace and independence to their lives.

"I'm still looking for an organization that will capture my imagination and need my support," she says, "but not my arms or my back!"

For more information, visit www.windfallbasics. com or write to Windfall, 29 Connell Court, Unit 3, Toronto, ON, M8Z 5T7, Canada.

STEPHANIE BOND

❧—IT'S NOT ABOUT THE DRESS—❧

Stephanie Bond grew up on a farm in east-
ern Kentucky, but traveled to distant lands
through stories between the covers of Harlequin romance novels. Years later, when Stephanie was several years into a corporate computer
programming career, the writing bug bit her,
and once again she turned to romance. In 1997
Stephanie left her corporate job to write wom-
en's fiction full-time. Her writing has brought
her full circle, allowing her to travel *in person*
to distant lands to teach workshops and pro-
mote her novels. To date she's written more
than forty wonderful projects for Harlequin,
such as short stories, novellas and full-length
novels, including a romantic mystery series
for the MIRA imprint called Body Movers. To
learn more about Stephanie Bond and her novels, visit: www.stephaniebond.com.

To my mother, Bonnie Bond,
for all that she does and for all that she is.

CHAPTER
∿ONE∿

CHLOE PARKER LOOKED in the mirror and her eyes welled with tears. "It's absolutely perfect." Melinda, the owner of Melinda's Bridal Shop, handed her a tissue and grabbed one for herself. "All the consultations, all the fittings, all the phone calls, all the times I wanted to fire you as a client—it was all worth it. You look like a fairy princess."

Chloe dabbed at her eyes and sighed at the reflection of the wedding gown that had been customized under her close supervision. Featuring a fitted bodice with delicate boning, a sweetheart neckline, short puff sleeves and a ballerina skirt with a six-foot-long train, the stunning garment had been fashioned from the finest Italian silk in a shade of white chosen specifically to complement her skin tone and dark hair. Clear Austrian crystals, each hand set and applied, sparkled from the full skirt, as well as the airy veil and matching silk mules.

It was the wedding dress that Chloe had dreamed of since she was a little girl—magical. The kind of dress that would set the mood for the wedding and for her marriage. How could any woman not be deliriously happy to walk down the aisle in this fanciful dress?

"I wish I could wear it every day until the wedding," she said with a sigh.

"What you do in your own apartment is your business," Melinda said slyly.

"No." Chloe shook her head. "I've waited this long, I can wait another twenty-one days."

Melinda picked up Chloe's left hand to study the sizable cluster of diamonds on her ring finger. "You're a lucky woman—the perfect dress *and* the perfect groom."

Chloe nodded in agreement. Dr. Ted Snyder was a sought-after cosmetic dentist, young and handsome, with impeccable manners and good breeding—not to mention amazing teeth. The engagement ring he'd had made for her still had tongues wagging in Toronto social circles—especially gratifying to Chloe, who had grown up outside of the "in" crowd.

"Everyone says your wedding is going to be the event of the year."

"That's my plan," Chloe said with a grin. From her bag her cell phone rang. She lifted the skirt of her dress and tiptoed over, leaning carefully so as not to wrinkle the silk, then pulled out her phone. "Chloe Parker Events Planning."

"Hi—this is Ann Conway."

Chloe glanced at her watch. "Hi, Ann. I'll be there in twenty minutes to double-check all the decorations for the birthday party and to meet the caterer. Is everything okay?"

"Actually, no. The magician just called to cancel."

Chloe frowned, but managed to inject a carefree tone into her voice. "I'm sure it's a mix-up of some kind, Ann. Just relax and I'll take care of everything." She disconnected the call, then consulted her day planner and punched in the phone number for Morton Green, aka Morton the Magnificent.

"Hello?"

"Hello, Morton, it's Chloe Parker."

"Chloe," he said, his voice squeaking nervously. "About the Conway boy's birthday party—"

"Morton, I told you never to cancel with a client directly."

"I'm sorry. I was afraid you'd be mad at me."

She could picture the middle-aged man cringing. "Wrong, Morton. I'm not mad because you're *not* canceling. I'll be at the Conways' house in twenty minutes, and you'd better have your magic butt there, too."

"Chloe, my assistant is sick—I can't go on without her."

"Then find someone else."

"Who am I going to find on such short notice?"

"That's your problem. I've never not delivered a

talent act for a party, and I'm not going to start today. My reputation is like gold to me."

"What size do you wear?" Morton asked.

"I beg your pardon?"

"If you can fit into the assistant's size-eight outfit, you can do the show with me."

"I don't think so."

"It's up to you," Morton said in a singsongy voice. "How far are you willing to go to preserve that fourteen-karat reputation of yours?"

Chloe screwed up her mouth, then rolled her eyes. "I draw the line at being sawed in half."

"See you there."

She disconnected, then sighed. It wasn't the first time she'd gone above and beyond the call of duty to preserve her standing as one of the top events planners in Toronto, and it probably wouldn't be the last. She took a last wistful look at herself in the glorious dress. "Melinda, will you unzip me? I have to run."

"At least this time you get to take the gown with you," the woman said.

"I know. I'm so excited just to be able to look at it whenever I want."

Melinda lowered the long back zipper. "You're not going to show it to Ted, are you?"

"I don't know. Maybe."

"You can't let the groom see the wedding gown before the wedding! It's bad luck."

Chloe gave a little laugh as Melinda eased the silk from her shoulders. "I'm not superstitious…but apparently I do believe in magic."

"Hmm?"

"Never mind. I have to go save a birthday party."

"That's why you're in demand," Melinda said, helping her step out of the garment. "I'll bag the dress, veil and shoes, and write up your final receipt."

Chloe couldn't help but notice that the woman was a little giddy, and nursed a fleeting pang of remorse for all the hoops she'd made Melinda jump through in this quest for the perfect dress. She suspected the woman would be glad to see her *and* the gown on their merry way.

After quickly dressing, Chloe emerged from the changing room and went to the counter to pay the final installment. The gown's hefty price tag reflected the time and effort put into the exquisite creation.

Melinda happily handed over Chloe's credit card and the receipt to sign, then jogged around the counter and took the bag down from the hook. "Allow me to carry it to your car."

"That's okay, I got it," Chloe said, slipping her finger through the hanger and holding it up high. "I'll miss seeing you, Melinda."

The seamstress pasted on a wide smile. "Good luck with your wedding."

Chloe strode to her van and hung the dress inside, feeling philosophical and unapologetic for the fuss she'd caused. Her wedding would be the feather in her cap, the best advertisement for her growing events coordinating business, an example of everything she could do for a client—from finding the most unique floral arrangements to the finest videographer to the most perfectly trained white doves to exit the church on cue. Her wedding would be proof that she would do almost anything to ensure a client's happiness.

She glanced at her watch, frustrated that she was going to be late. A delivery truck sat in front of her with its right signal on, waiting to turn. When the traffic light changed to green and the truck still didn't move, Chloe muttered, "Come on," and honked her horn loudly several times.

A long arm emerged from the driver's side, waving her around. She pulled up alongside the truck, which read Windfall Clothing Service, as the driver emerged from the cab to jump down and inspect a flat tire. Chloe felt a pang of regret for honking at his misfortune. He looked up as she drove slowly past, and she locked gazes with him.

Her stomach tingled as if she knew him, but there was nothing about his blond hair or rugged features that seemed recognizable. She didn't know anyone who drove a delivery truck, but maybe she'd seen him before on one of her jobs, transporting tables or chairs or a thousand other things. He smiled and gave her a friendly little wave. Odd, considering he had a flat in heavy Saturday traffic and would probably be late at his destination himself.

The car behind Chloe honked, jarring her out of her reverie. She continued on around the truck and made the turn. A few minutes later she pulled up to the Conways' house and saw that Morton the Magnificent was waiting for her, wearing a long black cape and a top hat. He grinned and held up a short, sequined outfit. Chloe heaved a resigned sigh. When she moved into Ted's house and into a bigger home office, she could hire her own assistant to do the tedious stuff. Meanwhile…

"Abracadabra," she murmured, then conjured up a bright smile and climbed out of her van.

THE CONWAY BOY's birthday party was a raging success, but ran longer than planned, so she was late meeting Ted for dinner. When she arrived at her apartment, he was sitting on the couch waiting for her, wearing neat chino pants, a long-sleeved dress shirt and a decided frown that deepened when he saw her sequined outfit. "What on earth are you wearing?"

"Long story," she said, tossing her purse and briefcase on the desk that took up most of the living room. She bent down for a quick kiss as she rushed by, carrying the bagged wedding gown. "Let me change. I'll be right out."

He glanced at his watch sourly. "Okay, but try to hurry. I didn't have lunch and I'm starving."

Once in her bedroom she hung the dress on her closet door. Ted had been impatient lately with her long hours at work and her preoccupation with the wedding details. Saturdays were usually more hectic, and sometimes she had back-to-back events. She told herself to make a special attempt to be more attentive during dinner, lest he start feeling neglected.

All would be forgiven the day of the wedding, though, when the most incredible production that Toronto had ever seen would unfold in front of five hundred lucky guests. Photographers from a bridal magazine and the *Toronto Star* would be in attendance to capture pictures of the twelve bridesmaids dressed in discriminating butter-yellow dresses, the tiny ballerinas who would spread flower petals as they danced and twirled down the aisle and the white-and-gold horse-drawn carriage that would carry her and Ted away to the elaborately decorated reception hall for a sit-down seafood dinner and dancing to a string quartet.

Chloe smiled to herself. Ted would thank her for making their day so special.

She glanced at the bagged wedding gown and bit her lip. Why not give him a preview? When Melinda's warning of bad luck flitted through her head, Chloe dismissed it as nonsense. All the phone calls, all the consultations, all the arrangements she'd made probably seemed abstract to Ted because she didn't have anything concrete to show him.

But the wedding dress—*that* he could understand.

She quickly changed into the gown, contorting to close the long back zipper and hook up the extensive train to form a bustle. She slid her feet into the matching shoes and attached the veil to her hair. Then, with heart pounding, she swept into the living room and waited for his reaction.

When he glanced up, he did a double take, his eyes wide, his mouth open. "Wh-what's this?"

"It's my dress, silly," she said with a laugh, turning in a circle for effect. "I picked it up today—what do you think? Isn't it amazing?"

He stood and nodded, his Adam's apple bouncing. Chloe was filled with feminine satisfaction that she'd managed to render him speechless.

"I thought I wasn't supposed to see it until the day of the wedding."

She gave a dismissive wave. "An old wives' tale. Won't it look wonderful with the yellow bridesmaids' dresses?" she asked, her excitement building. "And the charcoal-gray tuxedos? And the yellow lilies—"

"Chloe," he interrupted, his face pale. "I...I've changed my mind."

"About the dark gray tuxedos? Because we can still go with dove-gray if you want." She retrieved her cell phone from her purse and began punching in numbers. "I'll change it right now."

Ted snapped her phone closed. "I'm not talking about tuxedos, I'm talking about the wedding."

She frowned, then laughed. "What do you mean?"

"I mean the *wedding,* Chloe. I've changed my mind."

She shook her head. "I still don't understand. You've changed your mind about what?"

His jaw hardened. "I've changed my mind about marrying you. The wedding is off."

Chloe stood there, her mouth opening and closing. By the time Ted's words had sunk in, he was gone.

CHAPTER
~TWO~

CHLOE STOOD IN THE silent vacuum created by Ted leaving. He'd changed his mind about marrying her? Just like that? She ran after him, but her feet moved in slow motion because she was weighted down by the heavy dress. "Ted!" she yelled. "Wait! Ted!"

It was a struggle to fit through the door. She raced out onto the balcony of her second-floor apartment and searched for him in the parking lot below. He stood with his car door open, looking up at her. Some of her neighbors who happened to be outside walking pets and unloading groceries gaped at her, too.

"Ted, come back!" she called. "We can talk about this!"

But he only shook his head. "It's over, Chloe. I'm sorry." Then he climbed into his car and drove away.

Chloe stood there until she realized she was freezing in the spring chill and her neighbors were still staring up at her. What a sight she must make, standing there in a wedding gown, shouting after a man screeching away in his car.

She trudged back inside her apartment, hindered by the bulky dress and all that it symbolized. She closed the door and leaned against it, taking deep breaths, trying to make sense of what had just happened.

Ted had been distracted lately—irritable, even—but she'd attributed it to both of them being busy. Not once had she suspected he was having second thoughts about their marriage. Her heart squeezed painfully when the enormity of his rejection washed over her like a cold wave. She realized her cheeks were wet with tears, and hastily wiped at them before they fell and stained the gown.

As if it mattered. She looked down at the dress that she had so painstakingly selected and had tailored, the fairy-tale gown that was to be the centerpiece of her perfect showcase wedding and set the tone for her marriage. Suddenly, the hundreds of hand-set Austrian crystals mocked her. The yards of Italian silk suffocated her.

She couldn't get it off fast enough.

Of course, the zipper stuck. Chloe yelled in frustration, twisting around and giving it a hard yank before it finally gave way. She tore off the dress and tossed it on her bed, then kicked the silk shoes across the room. How could Ted do this to her?

Her panic ballooned as the arrangements that

would have to be canceled whirled through her mind—the church, the minister, the harpist, the soloist, the photographer, the videographer, the media, the dancers, the florist, the reception hall, the caterer, the string quartet, the limousine service, the hotel rooms, the gift registries, the horse-drawn carriage.

And the Hawaiian honeymoon…. She choked on a sob. After slaving over the details of the wedding for months, she had so been looking forward to two weeks of fun and sun to relax.

She drew a few shaky breaths, and her mind kicked into practical mode. There would be dozens of people to call—the bridesmaids, guests, her mother….

Her mother, who had raised Chloe by herself on few resources. Her mom, who was so proud of Chloe's successes and so happy that she was marrying well.

A new wave of tears swept over her. How would she tell her mother that she'd been dumped?

And she didn't even know why.

Sudden anger sparked in her belly, fanning to a flame. Chloe yanked up her cell phone and punched in Ted's number. After three years of dating and a year-long engagement, the very least he owed her was an explanation of why he would call off their wedding. How dare he humiliate her like this?

His phone rang and rang, and when it rolled over to his voice mail, she hung up and redialed. After five futile attempts, she threw down the phone and shouted in frustration. Incensed, she removed her engagement ring and bounced it off the wall, leaving a dent. She didn't see where the ring landed, didn't care. She paced, restless, overcome with the need to *do* something.

Chloe glanced at the clock. It was five-thirty on a Saturday afternoon. Most offices and retail stores would be closing soon; the calls to cancel the numerous arrangments for the wedding would have to wait until Monday.

When her gaze landed on the dress piled in a heap on the bed, she was overwhelmed with sadness. Her magical dress. She couldn't stand to look at it.

And if she hurried, she could return it before the bridal shop closed.

It was the one thread she could begin to unravel now, one proactive step to begin undoing all that she had put together over the past several months. One thing that would make her feel less helpless.

Resolved, Chloe stuffed the wedding gown, veil and shoes into the bag and raced to her van. She was numb on the short drive to the bridal shop, single-mindedly focused on getting the garment out of her sight.

Melinda was turning the Closed sign on her door when Chloe ran up, carrying the dress. The woman's eyes went wide and she tried to pretend she didn't see her, but Chloe pounded on the door until she relented and let her in.

"I'm returning the dress," Chloe said flatly. "The wedding is off."

Melinda looked incredulous. "What happened?"

She didn't want to admit that she should've heeded the warning about the groom seeing the bridal finery before the wedding. "Just take it," Chloe said tear-fully. "And get rid of it."

"But, Chloe, this is a custom gown. I can only give you back ten percent of what you paid for it."

"That's fine," she said, thinking something was better than nothing. She'd already be losing a fortune in deposits all over the city. She swallowed against the lump in her throat.

"I'm so sorry," Melinda said when she handed over the refund.

"Thanks," Chloe mumbled, her face flaming with embarrassment—a feeling she was going to have to get used to when word got out that Ted had dumped her.

She left the store and walked slowly to her van. Maybe Ted had decided he didn't want to marry someone who didn't have the pedigree of most of the people he hung out with. Or maybe he'd met someone else. Chloe climbed into the vehicle and sat with her hands on the steering wheel for several minutes, dreading the thought of going back to her apartment. Her empty stomach rumbled, reminding her of the dinner with Ted she was supposed to be having. Across the street, the sign of an ice cream shop beckoned.

She'd been watching her weight for the sake of looking good in that darn dress, which now was a moot point, so why not?

Chloe parked the van, then went inside and ordered a carton of strawberry-chocolate-cheesecake ice cream. When the worker extended napkins, as well as a tiny wooden spoon, across the counter, Chloe shook her head. "I'm going to need a bigger spoon."

The guy's eyebrows furrowed but he obliged, handing over what looked like a wooden paddle.

She was digging in before she drove away. The chocolate, caffeine, sugars and fats hit her system like a drug, the ultimate in self-medication. She moaned in contentment and noted that Ben & Jerry's was missing out on an I Was Dumped Devil's Food flavor of ice cream.

By the time she got home, the container was empty, her stomach hurt and her heart ached. All around her apartment were pictures of her and Ted, reminders of the life they'd planned together. How had things gone so wrong so quickly? And why hadn't she seen it coming?

Then a terrifying thought sent alarm spiraling through her: how many people had Ted already told? Had he called her mother? His family? His friends? *Her* friends? The notion sent her running to the bathroom, where she emptied the contents of her upset stomach into the commode. She emerged somewhat calmer, reasoning that if he'd told people, they would've called her, and her cell phone remained silent.

But she wouldn't be able to wait much longer before she started making the calls.

She tried to think of someone to phone for support, but just wasn't ready to bare her soul. Humiliation coursed through her like a toxin, burning her from the inside out.

After slowly lowering herself to the floor in front of the couch, she hugged her knees, seized by the irrational thought that if she remained very still, perhaps time would, as well. But as she sat in the silence reliving the surreal one-sided conversation that had left her a jilted bride, evening shadows fell across her living room, across her arms and legs. Evening turned into night, and when she dragged herself up to go to bed, her limbs were stiff. The sharp pain of Ted's rebuff had turned into a constant ache. Her eyes and throat were swollen and raw. Her head pounded. Her stomach was leaden.

She fell onto her bed, hoping for the quick release of sleep, but no such luck. She tossed and turned as she played out what would happen in the coming days…weeks…months…years. Dismantling the wedding would be a Herculean effort, but it was nothing compared with this feeling of having her heart ripped out and stomped on. She'd had glimpses of Ted's casual dismissal of certain things and even some people, but she'd never dreamed that she would be on the receiving end of his alienation.

He'd said he loved her. Wanted to spend the rest of his life with her….

Chloe turned over, looking for a cool spot on her damp pillow. Would she be considered damaged goods? Many of her customers were wealthy acquaintances of Ted's; she relied on their referrals to keep her business afloat. Would they withdraw their support when they found out that one of their own had tossed her aside?

And the word *why?* kept hammering away in her head.

Somewhere toward dawn, she began to tell herself all the practical things she'd heard on talk shows. It was better to find out before the wedding versus afterward. You couldn't make someone love you. If Ted didn't recognize what a catch she was, then it was his loss.

But the platitudes did little to assuage the abject mortification of being so heartlessly discarded.

As light began to filter into her bedroom, Chloe finally dozed, but was jarred awake what seemed like only minutes later by a piercing sound. She sat straight up, disoriented, before realizing that her cell phone alarm was going off. As she searched for it groggily, the events of the previous evening came crashing back—along with a splintering headache. When she found the phone, she pushed her hair out of her eyes to read the display.

REMINDER: SHALE BRUNCH AT 10.

Chloe groaned. She'd forgotten about Mindy Shale's bridal shower brunch. Of all days to have to coordinate a wedding-related event, and to top it off, Mindy Shale was a friend of Ted's sister, Jenna.

Chloe put her hand to her throbbing head and wondered if they knew yet about Ted dumping her. She could beg off with a phone call, say she wasn't feeling well. Check in with the hotel banquet director and the caterer via phone to make sure everything was in place.

Then she gave herself a mental shake. She'd never skipped out on an event that she'd coordinated, and she didn't plan to start now. If Ted's friends were inclined to take their patronage elsewhere, it was even more important that she give this party her best shot and attract new clients.

But she almost changed her mind about going when she saw her reflection in the mirror. She hadn't bothered to remove her makeup the night before, and it was smeared and streaked from tears and sleep. Her dark hair was a rat's nest from tossing and turning. And her eyes were nearly swollen shut. If Ted could see her now, he'd be thanking his lucky stars that he'd backed out of the wedding.

That almost made her smile—which was the first glimmer of hope she'd had that she might get through this ordeal intact. So she downed a couple of aspirin for the headache, took a bracing cold shower to rejuvenate and spent twice her usual time applying makeup to camouflage the effects of an all-night crying jag.

The result wasn't half-bad, she acknowledged. She put on a bright floral dress and pink shoes and made it to the hotel forty-five minutes before the start of the shower. After smoothing out a couple of problems, tweaking the table decorations and test-tasting items on the menu, she took photos to add to her scrapbook and was ready to greet Mindy Shale and friends when they arrived.

Mindy was blond and perky and reeked of money, as did all of her friends. They were the same age as Chloe, but they seemed so much more worldly, she thought with envy. Most of them had traveled abroad and gone to prestigious universities. Their parents were physicians or attorneys or politicians. She felt a bit like a servant hovering on the periphery, answering questions and fetching things for Mindy, but it took her mind off Ted.

Until his sister arrived.

Chloe and Jenna's relationship had always been amiable, but at times Chloe thought she detected a faint air of disapproval from Jenna, as if she wanted Chloe to know that even if she married Ted, she wouldn't truly belong to their social circle. When the young woman said hello, Chloe tried to act natural, but could feel her face warming. Did Jenna know? She and Ted were close, so it seemed reasonable that he would've told her he'd called off the wedding.

But Jenna's expression remained cool and impassive, as always. Whatever secrets she knew about her brother, she wasn't revealing them. Chloe put on her best professional face and went about handling details of the brunch while trying to hide her ringless left hand. The only time she came close to losing her cool was when she thought of her own shower brunch, which was supposed to take place in one week at this very hotel.

Yet another set of phone calls to make.

She blinked back the threat of tears and somehow made it through the event with her smile intact.

Mindy seemed pleased with the outcome and especially with the party favors, blown-glass perfume bottles that Chloe had found at an exclusive boutique.

"I'll recommend you to all my friends," the bride-to-be gushed.

Chloe thanked her, and as she walked to her van, muttered under her breath that she hoped the woman felt the same after she discovered Chloe had been dumped by Ted. And everyone would know soon because she intended to start making those dreaded phone calls when she got back to her place.

"Hello, Chloe."

She looked up and almost stumbled to see Ted leaning against her van, his hands in his pockets.

"What are you doing here?" she asked, her pulse thumping.

"I came to see you," he said simply. "I remembered you were coordinating Mindy's shower, and when Jenna mentioned she was attending... Well, I thought this would be a neutral place to talk."

Chloe crossed her arms. "To talk about what?"

He looked sheepish. "To talk about what an idiot I am."

Hope fluttered in her chest, but the anger still lingered. "I'm listening."

He pushed himself from the van and lifted his hands in the air. "When I saw you wearing the wedding dress, I just panicked. I guess I got cold feet, and I didn't handle it well. I want to marry you, Chloe."

She wavered, near tears and exhausted from a sleepless night. A tiny part of her asked how, if he loved her, he could put her through something so ghastly. But another part of her whispered that it was her fault for springing the wedding dress on him unexpectedly when he was already in a bad mood. It had blindsided him, spooked him.

"Can you forgive me?" he asked.

They'd lost less than twenty-four hours—a minuscule lapse compared to the rest of their life together. Chloe smiled. "Yes." Then she went into his arms for a makeup kiss. She closed her eyes and squeezed him, telling herself that eventually the hurt would subside and everything would feel perfect again.

He clasped her hand. "Where's your ring?"

"At my apartment," she said, reluctant to tell him that she'd bounced it off her bedroom wall. "I'll put it on as soon as I get home."

"Good. Did you tell anyone about my stupidity?"

She shook her head. "I guess I was hoping you'd change your mind."

Ted smiled. "I'm just glad I came to my senses before you pulled the plug on the entire wedding."

The dress. Chloe winced, wishing she hadn't acted so impulsively in returning it. The bridal shop was closed Sundays, but no matter, she thought happily—she'd get it first thing tomorrow morning. Melinda would be relieved.

"THE DRESS ISN'T HERE, CHLOE."

Chloe leaned forward on the counter. "Melinda, how can the dress not be here? I brought it back Saturday as you were closing, and now you're just re-opening."

Melinda turned pale and wrung her hands. "You told me to get rid of it."

A finger of alarm tickled Chloe's spine. "Melinda, where *is* my wedding dress?"

"I gave it to a charity, along with a truckload of other gowns."

Chloe's throat convulsed. "You gave away my wedding gown?" She grabbed the lapels on the woman's jacket. "I'm getting married in less than three weeks—I have to have that dress!"

Melinda cringed. "I'm sorry, Chloe. A couple of times a year I give leftover stock to an organization that distributes clothing to the needy." She rummaged behind the counter and came up with a brochure, which she extended to Chloe with a shaking hand.

Shell-shocked, Chloe took the brochure and read the name of the organization, Windfall Clothing Service. The words strummed a memory chord and she had to think for a few seconds before she recalled the delivery truck with the flat tire. And the handsome driver. What a strange coincidence.

"When was the dress picked up?" Chloe asked.

"Saturday evening after I closed."

So chances were good that it was still sitting in a truck somewhere, perhaps at the organization's office, or in a warehouse. She glanced at the address on the brochure and headed toward the door.

"Chloe, where are you going?" Melinda called.

"To find my wedding dress!" she shouted.

CHAPTER
∽THREE∽

Chloe lifted her gaze from the brochure and stared at the entrance to the Windfall Clothing Service office. The organization had been founded by two women who recognized the opportunity to redirect clothes and other basic-need items that manufacturers and retailers wanted to clear out. Agencies would then distribute them to the homeless, those displaced by natural disasters, and refugees from other countries, among others.

Guilt plucked at her heartstrings. This organization was doing wonderful things for many people, marrying resources to need. She felt embarrassed to go in and admit she was there to take back an expensive wedding dress that had been inadvertently donated after her fiancé had called off the wedding, which was now back on. Her problem seemed petty in light of the work that Windfall was doing.

Although…perhaps she could make a donation to offset the time and trouble it would take to locate her dress. Feeling better, Chloe climbed out of her van and entered the office.

An attractive brunette standing next to a file cabinet smiled at her. "Welcome to Windfall. I'm Terri. How can I help you?"

Through a large window behind the desk Chloe caught a glimpse of a vast warehouse bustling with workers and filled with pallet after pallet of clothing and other items. The sheer magnitude of merchandise that the organization dealt with began to dawn on Chloe, making her dilemma seem even smaller in comparison.

She manufactured a smile. "My name is Chloe Parker. I heard about your organization through a retail store owner who donates clothing."

The woman nodded. "We have so many wonderful retail contributors. Which one?"

"Melinda's Bridal Shop on Queen Street?"

"Oh, yes, of course. It sounds strange, I know, donating gowns and formal wear to the needy, but there are people out there who are grateful for the chance to celebrate happy events with a special dress they couldn't otherwise afford."

Chloe swallowed miserably. "How nice."

"What can I do for you?" Terri asked cheerfully.

"I…" Feeling trapped by her own selfishness and looking for a way out, Chloe glanced around the office, her gaze landing on a sign that read, We Always Need Volunteers. Her mind raced furiously. There was nothing she wouldn't do to satisfy a client, and right now, she was her own client. If she volunteered to work for the organization, maybe she could secretly look for her gown. It was probably somewhere in that warehouse, waiting to be sorted and distributed locally.

She just needed to buy a little time until she could find it. And if she volunteered, she wouldn't feel so bad about what she was doing. Everybody won.

"I'd like to volunteer my time to Windfall," Chloe said impulsively.

"Oh, wonderful! We can't have enough volunteers." Terri gestured for her to sit, and pulled out a form. Dropping into the chair behind the desk, she began filling in Chloe's background, references and contact information. "Do you have any special skills you'd like to share?"

"I run an events-planning company, so I'm very organized." She withdrew a business card and extended it across the desk.

Terri took it, nodding. "Great. We can always use help here in the office and in the warehouse. Routing the clothes to the proper outlets takes a lot of coordination, especially in peak times, such as emergencies."

"Sounds perfect for me," Chloe said, nodding in turn.

"How many hours a week would you like to volunteer?"

"I was thinking a couple of hours a day for now."

"Would it be possible to work mornings?"

"Actually, early mornings are best for me," Chloe said, relieved that she wouldn't have to juggle her regular work schedule. "From seven to nine?"

"Great. The office will already be unlocked, although there might not be very many people here at that time."

All the better, Chloe thought.

"I see you have our brochure." Terri nodded to the paper sticking out of Chloe's purse. "There's more information on our website, too, if you'd like to know the full spectrum of what we do here at Windfall."

"I'll check it out," she promised.

"Good. Then I just have one more question," the woman said with a grin. "When can you start?"

"How about tomorrow morning?"

"Perfect. Would you like a tour?"

"Sure." The sooner she learned the logistics of the business, the better.

When the door to the warehouse opened, Chloe looked up and blinked in surprise to see the blond man who'd been driving the truck with the flat. He walked in studying a piece of paper, which he laid on the corner of Terri's desk, some sort of list. When he looked up, he glanced over at her and tilted his head, as if trying to place her.

Chloe squirmed, hoping he didn't remember she'd been the driver blasting her horn.

"Hi, Andy," Terri said. "Meet Chloe Parker— she's a new volunteer."

"Hello," he said, giving her a friendly smile. "I'm Andy Shearer."

She smiled back, a little dismayed at the way her pulse accelerated. He was a big guy, with broad shoulders and an earthy appearance that made her think of hiking and camping, things she hadn't done since she was a child. "Nice to meet you," she murmured.

The phone rang and Terri excused herself. After a few seconds, she covered the mouthpiece. "Sorry, I need to take this. Andy, I was about to give Chloe a tour. Would you mind showing her around?"

"Not at all," he said smoothly, opening the door and sweeping his arm in front of him. "After you, Chloe."

She walked past him and a shiver of awareness traveled over her shoulders. He had deep blue eyes, pale lashes and freckles on his tanned cheeks. His dark blond hair was short and thick, glinting with golden highlights from the sun. His shirtsleeves were rolled up past brown, muscular forearms. His faded jeans were low slung and molded powerful thighs. His work boots were scuffed and worn. He was… what was the word?

Hot.

"Are you okay?" he asked, flashing white teeth.

"I'm fine," she said, picking up the pace and chiding herself for observing the man's physical assets. Considerable as they were, it wasn't like her to notice other men. She was engaged, after all, mere weeks away from tying the knot. And she was here on a mission—to find her wedding gown. Not to ogle the help.

He was squinting at her. "Have we met before?"

Chloe's stomach did a little flip. "I don't think so."

"You seem familiar to me for some reason."

"I m-must have one of those faces," she stammered.

"One of those nice ones," he said, nodding.

Her cheeks warmed with a blush. "Thank you." She averted her gaze, trying to focus on the matter at hand rather than the disconcerting man next to her.

"This, as you can tell," he said, gesturing to the noisy scene in front of them, "is the warehouse. Donors either deliver items to us or we pick them up. Everything comes here to be sorted and bundled for distribution to agencies and shelters all over Toronto."

The warehouse was as big as a football field, and every section of it bustled with activity. Chloe looked at the mountains of clothing and boxes that workers were picking through and her stomach sank. Her dress could be anywhere. It would be like looking for a needle in a haystack.

Granted, a white, sparkly needle, but still....

"It's a little overwhelming," she said, surveying the goings-on.

"So is the need," Andy remarked. "This organization has grown from a small operation to a vital source of aid in our community."

"I had no idea," Chloe murmured, feeling humbled.

"So what brings you to Windfall?"

She pulled a half-truth from thin air. "I...heard about the organization...and wanted to...help."

Maybe she should just come clean and admit why she was there and ask for their help in finding the dress.

"I'm sure Terri is thrilled to have an extra body."

His gaze traveled down her legs, and the chilly warehouse suddenly seemed overheated. It occurred to Chloe that he was flirting with her…and she was enjoying it. She looked everywhere but at him.

Andy cleared his throat. "And what do you do when you aren't volunteering, Chloe?"

"I own an events-coordinating business."

His eyebrows went up. "You plan parties?"

Chloe bristled. Why did it sound frivolous when he said it? "Yes. And other…events."

"Sounds interesting," he said, his eyes dancing. "And a nice way to spend your days—making people happy."

She smiled. "That's the general idea."

"You have a nice smile. You should use it more often."

She held his gaze for a few seconds until an alarm sounded in her head. *This man is dangerous to your peace of mind.* Instead of responding, she glanced away and resumed walking. But she was ultra-aware of him walking beside her.

They toured all around the warehouse, with Andy pointing out steps of the operation along the way. Chloe scanned every pile of clothing for a flash of white, sparkly fabric, not sure what she would do if she spotted something. But as it turned out, she didn't see anything resembling her dress. The air was full of dust and lint. Part of their job, he pointed out, was opening packages and removing labels from the clothing before it went out to various agencies.

"Cutting out the labels protects the donors," he said, "so no one can return the items to a store for a refund."

"How long does it take for the items to be processed, from pickup to delivery?"

He shrugged. "Depending on the demand, as little as a few hours to maybe a week or two."

"Depending on the demand?"

"Coats in winter, kids' clothes and backpacks when school starts, that kind of thing. We try to be as responsive as possible, given our constraints."

Chloe nodded. Andy had a pleasing, natural way of speaking and carrying himself. He was, she decided, a good ambassador for the organization. But he unnerved her with the way he looked at her—as if he was trying to figure her out. And she felt as if her ulterior motive for being here was written all over her face. To her relief, they were soon back where they'd started.

"Thank you for the tour," she said, edging toward the office door, eager to put distance between her and his perceptive blue eyes.

Andy nodded, then put his hands on his hips. "Look, I'm not one for beating around the bush. Are you single, Chloe Parker?"

She was so taken aback by his forthrightness that for a few seconds she lost her voice…and her memory. Then she recalled the reason she was here. "Actually, I'm engaged to be married," she said finally.

He looked at her left hand. "Sorry, I didn't see a ring."

"It's at home," she said, slightly irritated. She hadn't been able to find her engagement ring, and she needed to before she saw Ted again. "I always wear it…usually."

He looked amused. "And have you set a date for your walk down the aisle?"

"Three weeks from this past Saturday," Chloe said, feeling defensive.

Andy winked at her. "Too bad. Nice meeting you." Then he gave her a little salute and walked away.

Chloe frowned at the man's broad back. Too bad? Whatever happened to "good luck"?

ANDY SHEARER WALKED AWAY, fighting the urge to look back for another glimpse of Chloe Parker. When he'd walked into the office and seen her, he'd felt as if he'd been sucker punched. The woman was beautiful, with her big brown eyes, full pink lips and masses of dark wavy hair pulled back with a prim yellow ribbon. And there was something about her….

He shook his head, wondering why someone like her was volunteering for Windfall. He liked to give people the benefit of the doubt, but his gut told him that something wasn't on the up-and-up here.

Then he sighed. No matter the motivation, a volunteer was a volunteer, so it would be nice to have Chloe around. But he planned to keep an eye on her…a task he was looking forward to, despite the fact that she'd been quick to tell him she was to be married soon.

Because there was something fishy going on with this woman, and he intended to find out what.

CHAPTER
∼FOUR∼

CHLOE HID A YAWN behind her hand, a result of her early morning wake-up, and flipped through the pile of papers in front of her, looking for any mention of a delivery pickup from Melinda's Bridal Shop. "These receipts are from two weeks ago," she announced.

"We're running a little behind," Terri said, "but working at a good pace. See these account numbers listed at the bottom of the receipts? Each one represents an agency that received a parcel of the clothes or items on that receipt. In other words, all of the things listed on this receipt have already been distributed. We just have to make sure the paperwork accurately reflects what was taken and what was sent out or retained."

"Retained?"

"That means it couldn't be shipped out for some

reason—maybe it was out of season or in disrepair, a pair of shoes was mismatched, or something like that."

"Wow, you keep a close eye on what comes in and what goes out," Chloe remarked, thinking that even if she found her wedding dress, she'd still have to figure out a way to get it out of there. According to Andy's information, unless the agencies experienced a sudden demand for wedding gowns, she had less than two weeks to find the dress.

But if they were two weeks behind processing paperwork in the office, the dress would be gone by the time the receipt from Melinda's Bridal Shop crossed her desk.

"Our funding depends on good record keeping," Terri said, breaking into Chloe's thoughts. "We'd rather be slow and accurate."

"Are employees and volunteers allowed to take clothes home?"

Terri shook her head. "The donated items are strictly for clients."

"Are they allowed to buy things?"

Again, the woman shook her head. "It's important that no one has the opportunity to profit from the items that are donated to Windfall. We have signed contracts with our agencies that they will provide clothing free of charge to those in need."

It was a simple, effective idea, Chloe acknowledged—matching manufacturer and retailer overstock to agencies through a clearinghouse that ensured the items went where they were most needed. The donors received tax write-offs on products that might otherwise wind up in landfills; the agencies and shelters received much-needed items to satisfy the ever-increasing demand. Even more remarkable, the organization relied solely on private donations and fund-raising events.

"How long have you been working here?" Chloe asked Terri.

"About eight years now. Every year Windfall has grown, and unfortunately, so has the need."

Terri appeared to be one of a handful of full-time employees, and the woman was dedicated to Windfall. It was clear she put in more hours than a standard workweek simply out of love for the organization.

Chloe continued sorting invoices by date. "How long has Andy been here?"

"That's a good question. I'm not sure—he was here when I started, and it seems as if he's always around."

The door to the office opened and Terri said, "Speak of the devil."

Chloe looked up to see the man whose face had plagued her dreams last night. Today he was dressed in jeans and a navy sweatshirt that reflected the blue in his eyes. He gave them a wicked grin. "My ears were burning, so I thought I'd come in to eavesdrop."

Terri laughed and waved him off. "Chloe was asking how long you've been here, and I couldn't tell her."

"Hmm." He looked up to the ceiling. "I guess it's been about ten years now."

Admirable, Chloe conceded, because she knew the man couldn't make much money driving a delivery truck for Windfall. Maybe he was the kind of guy who wanted a flexible, low-pressure job to give him time for other pursuits.

Unlike Ted, who tended to operate at extremes. He put in long workweeks, and on weekends, he preferred a drink in one hand and a TV remote control in the other. He didn't have many interests outside his dental practice and his friends...and Chloe. His career was his top priority, but it would afford them a very comfortable life together.

"How's the first day going?" Andy asked Chloe.

"She's doing great," Terri enthused.

"Just trying to learn my way around," Chloe said.

He nodded, but seemed to study her. Then he threw up his hand and backed toward the door. "Gotta make a delivery. Have a good one, ladies."

When the door closed behind him, Chloe felt Terri's gaze on her.

"Andy's cute," Terri offered.

"I hadn't noticed," she replied.

"And he's single."

"But I'm not," Chloe murmured, hiding her bare left hand. Even though she'd torn her bedroom apart, she still hadn't found her engagement ring.

She excused herself to visit the washroom, which happened to be in the warehouse. Chloe tried to seem casual as she checked for any sign of Andy, but the man wasn't around. Relieved, she took the long way to the washroom, scanning the pallets of clothes for anything that resembled formal wear or dress bags. She smiled at the gloved workers sorting things, and tried to look as if she belonged there.

"Searching for something?"

At the sound of Andy's voice, Chloe froze between two mountains of what looked to be women's pajamas. She turned around and smiled. "Yes—the washroom."

He pointed to the opposite end of the warehouse. "Over there."

She nodded. "Okay...thanks. I thought you were going out on a delivery."

"The truck wasn't loaded yet."

"Oh. Well, thanks." She moved to step past him.

"I see you're still not wearing your engagement ring," he said, nodding to her hand.

Annoyance flashed through her. "It's...being cleaned."

"Gee, it must be a big one if it takes that long."

She gritted her teeth. "It is."

He smiled and gave her his signature salute. "See you later."

Chloe walked away, frustrated. How was she ever going to find her dress with that man seemingly stalking her every move?

Andy watched the lovely Chloe retreat. The plot thickened.

CHLOE SETTLED INTO a routine of working with Terri in the office from seven to nine every morning and sneaking away whenever possible to walk up and down the aisles of donated items. She was feeling a little desperate by the end of the week, when she still hadn't seen any sign of inventory from Melinda's shop. She hoped it was still at the bottom of one of the pallets, waiting to be processed.

She'd been working furiously on the receipts in the office, catching up to only a three-day lag from when the clothes left the warehouse. She continued to ask questions about the process, trying to figure out how she might circumvent the paperwork and find out where the dresses had been stored in the massive warehouse. But as near as she could tell, the receipt she was looking for must be in one of the stacks that the couple of dozen warehouse assistants maintained at their stations. And she couldn't very well go around asking to riffle through them all.

"Would it be all right if I collected receipts from the warehouse assistants?" Chloe asked on Friday morning.

Terri looked up. "They usually just drop them off when they have a pile."

"I know, but I was thinking I might come in tomorrow and try to get caught up."

Terri smiled. "That's not necessary. We've learned to accept that we're always going to be a little behind in the office."

"I'd like to," Chloe pressed.

The woman shrugged. "Okay. You're amazing. I hope you decide to stay around here."

Chloe felt a twinge of guilt, but told herself that

her motivation wasn't important—she was doing work that needed to be done. That was what mattered.

Wasn't it?

Meanwhile, she scrupulously avoided Andy Shearer whenever possible, which wasn't easy. The man was everywhere. Anytime he saw her in the warehouse, he approached her and struck up a conversation. Worse, he kept staring at her left hand.

And she still hadn't found her darn ring. Tomorrow after leaving Windfall and running errands, she intended to tear apart her bedroom before her dinner date with Ted. She'd been able to avoid explaining the ring's absence only because they were both so busy getting their affairs in order before leaving for their honeymoon, they'd barely had a chance to talk, much less see each other. If she got lucky, maybe she'd find her dress *and* the ring tomorrow. Then everything would be perfect again.

She entered the warehouse and began going around to the assistants to collect receipts. "Just trying to get a jump on the paperwork," she explained to each one. "By the way, a friend of mine who runs a bridal shop donates to Windfall—do you remember any wedding dresses coming in lately?"

The warehouse assistants spent the entire day on their feet, moving between the loading docks, instructing forklift operators where to drop their load and continually trying to stay on top of all the sorting, plus packing outgoing pallets to meet the various agencies' requirements. Despite the harried environment, each of them took the time to greet her and respond kindly to her not-so-innocent question, once again dredging up guilty feelings in Chloe for imposing on their time. She'd already spoken to half of them, but no one remembered logging in a shipment of wedding gowns.

"Looks like you could use a hand."

Chloe closed her eyes and swallowed a bad word. Then she turned and smiled brightly at Andy. "No, thanks."

Ignoring her response, he took the armload of papers from her and proceeded to follow her around as she collected receipts from other assistants, his big ears effectively thwarting her attempt to ask questions.

"You must be getting caught up in the office," he commented. "Terri can't say enough about how wonderful your work is."

"She's just glad to have an extra set of hands," Chloe said, feeling her blood pressure rise at his proximity. Why did the man have to be so...observant?

"Speaking of hands—I'm dying to see this gigantic engagement ring of yours. Are you saving it for a special occasion?"

Chloe frowned. "Don't you have something to do?"

He grinned. "Nothing more interesting."

She turned her back and collected a sheaf of papers from the next assistant. "I'm not that interesting."

"I disagree," he said smoothly.

Chloe glanced at her watch. "Oh, look at the time. I have to go."

"Planning any good parties today?" he asked, following her back toward the office.

"As a matter of fact, I am—my bridal brunch is on Sunday," she said pointedly.

"Sounds like a blast. Are all your friends as high society as you?"

Chloe stopped and looked up at him, thinking he'd be surprised to know that she came from very modest means, that her entrée into high society had been recent and by way of Ted and her fledgling business. Andy's arrogance infuriated her.

"You don't know me," she said, her chest rising and falling. "You don't know anything about me."

"But I'd like to."

His words sent a warm tickle to her stomach. The thought *I'd like to get to know you, too,* floated through her head until she realized the insanity of the notion. Exasperated at her response to him, she said, "Are you deaf? I'm getting married in two weeks."

"Don't you have any room in your life for another friend?"

Chloe considered the man before her and tamped down the confusing emotions churning within her. He was maddening. And the way her pulse picked up when he was nearby eliminated the possibility that they could ever just be friends. Besides, she didn't plan to be at Windfall any longer than necessary.

She reached out and took the papers he was carrying, adding them to her considerable stack. "I have all the friends I need," she said, and walked back into the office.

Terri glanced up at her. "Is everything okay between you and Andy?"

"Fine," Chloe said, putting down the receipts she planned to tackle tomorrow and picking up her purse. "Have a good day."

CHAPTER
∽FIVE∽

CHLOE WAS EAGER to get to Windfall the next morning, eager to ask the rest of the warehouse assistants if they were aware of a wedding-gown shipment, and then go through all the receipts she'd collected the previous day. A slow drip of panic had begun to remind her that she had only two weeks left to find her wedding gown. She simply couldn't fathom walking down the aisle wearing anything else.

Terri wasn't coming in today, so upon arriving, Chloe sat in the quiet office and sifted through the receipts, her heart pounding. When she reached the last one, she heaved a sigh of relief. No receipt from the bridal shop with outgoing agency codes meant that chances were good the wedding gown was still somewhere in the warehouse.

The place was abuzz with activity this morning as

more volunteers arrived. Which allowed her to mingle and move among the mounds of clothing without drawing too much attention to the fact that she was checking every section like a dog on the hunt.

"I didn't expect to see you here today."

Chloe stopped and swallowed a groan. Then she turned to face her handsome tormentor. "Likewise."

Andy smiled widely, as if he knew that he got on her nerves and enjoyed it. "I see you've left the office to lend a hand out here."

"Just trying to learn more about the organization," she said breezily.

"Really? Would you like to see what happens to all these things?"

"What do you mean?"

He jerked his thumb toward a loading dock where a truck sat. "I'm getting ready to make a delivery. Why don't you come with me?"

Alone with him in close quarters? "I don't know," she hedged.

"Come on, I could use an extra hand." His eyes were warm and hopeful.

How was it possible that someone so maddening could be so irresistible? "Okay," she heard herself say, even though she felt as if she were entering a hazardous zone.

He grinned. "Great. Let's go."

She followed him to the truck self-consciously and allowed him to help her climb into the seat. His big hands felt warm and capable on her arm and waist. A jolt of awareness warmed her all over. He smiled and winked before closing the door, then walked around and bounded into his own seat.

"Buckle up."

She pulled the seat belt over her shoulder. "Where are we going?"

"To a community center to give out toys. Vaccinations are being administered, and the kids are generally more willing to come if they can take home something to play with."

Chloe nodded and concentrated on the passing streetscape. "So you come in on Saturdays, too?"

"Most of the time. I thought Saturdays would be busy for you, with parties and all."

"I've cut back a little to have time to get ready for my wedding," she said, mentioning it as much as a reminder for herself as for him.

"Oh, right—the wedding. Is it going to be a big to-do?" Then he laughed. "Since you're a party planner, I guess so, huh?"

"I suppose. It's something I've always dreamed of."

He grinned. "That's where men and women are different."

"You don't want to get married?" she asked drily.

"Oh, sure, someday," he said, surprising her with his enthusiasm. "I guess I've always dreamed about the bride, though, instead of the ceremony."

Chloe hesitated a moment, then said, "So tell me about your bride."

He shrugged. "I guess she's more of an idea than

a face, but if I had to describe her, I'd say pretty, of course, with a great smile."

He threw Chloe a meaningful glance and she smiled in spite of herself.

"Kind and generous," he continued, "and flexible."

She frowned. "That's a little pervy."

He laughed out loud, a pleasing rumbling sound. "I meant flexible in terms of her attitude—willing to adapt."

Chloe squirmed, wondering if he was going down his checklist of desirable traits in a woman for her benefit, implying that she wasn't "flexible." Not that it mattered. Then she frowned. Did Ted have a checklist? Did she?

"And you'll know this woman when you see her?" Chloe asked.

He nodded confidently. "I have good instincts when it comes to sizing up people."

There was that look again, as if he could peer directly into her dishonest heart and see the reason she had volunteered at Windfall. Chloe opened her mouth to confess, but realized suddenly that she didn't want this man to think poorly of her.

"What does your fiancé do?" he asked.

Safer ground. "He's a dentist."

He grinned. "I'll bet he has perfect teeth."

Chloe shifted in her seat. How could he make something positive sound so frivolous, as if that was Ted's best quality?

"Here we are," he said, wheeling into a parking lot and driving to a far corner to bring the truck to a halt.

Chloe jumped down from the seat before he could come around to help her. She didn't like the way she was starting to feel toward Andy, or the way he was making her feel about herself and her upcoming wedding. The man had a propensity to turning things on end.

He unhooked the back door of the truck and lifted it, causing the muscles in his arms to bunch in a most desirable way. Chloe looked away and chastised herself. She shouldn't have come.

"I'm glad you came," he said, as if he could read her mind. "The kids always react better when there's a woman around." He winked. "Me, too."

She couldn't help but laugh as he handed down net bags of toys and stuffed animals. She felt a little like Santa when they walked into the community center. The waiting room was crammed with small children, many of them sitting on their mothers' laps or clinging to their knees. It was clear that most of them knew today's visit involved some kind of needle, and they were under duress. Chloe's heart squeezed for them.

But their expressions changed when they realized they could choose a toy from the many bags Chloe and Andy brought in. When Chloe extended a small doll to a shy little girl wearing a clean but shabby dress, a repressed memory slid into her head. She'd been a little girl much like this one, sitting on her mother's lap, waiting to see the doctor. And someone had given her a toy—a colorful windmill on a stick that spun when she blew on it.

Chloe straightened and blinked back tears. Until this moment, she hadn't realized the toy was charity; she only remembered how much better it had made her feel. She and her mother had benefited from an organization much like Windfall….

"Hey, are you okay?" Andy asked, looking suddenly concerned.

"I'm fine," she said, hastily wiping her eyes.

"You're crying."

"I said I'm fine," she repeated, more vehemently than she'd planned.

Andy's expression gentled. He pulled a tissue from a box sitting on a nearby counter and handed it to her, then smiled at the next waiting child. Chloe took the tissue and dabbed at the corners of her eyes, watching Andy interact with the little ones. His comment about kids responding better to women didn't seem to be true where he was concerned. Despite his large size, the children gravitated to him and squealed in delight as he pretended to steal noses with his thumb and wiggled his ears for them. Chloe felt her heart lurch sideways. Whenever Andy found the woman he'd been dreaming of, he would make a wonderful father. And he was the kind of man a woman would want to have babies with. He just seemed so genuine and full of life.

She steered her runaway thoughts back to Ted. They hadn't resolved to have children, but hadn't ruled it out, either. Both of them were just so busy in their careers, they had decided to postpone the matter until later, when they'd settled into married life. In retrospect, Chloe realized the decision had been somewhat clinical. Why didn't looking at Ted make her think of freckle-faced children?

She arranged her face in a smile, but troubling thoughts pecked at her as she and Andy finished passing out the toys. To his credit, he didn't ask her any more about the sudden tears, didn't tease her again about her impending wedding. When they returned to the warehouse, he was friendly, but seemed more cautious around her.

"Thanks for asking me to go with you," she ventured.

"Thank you for going."

"I…enjoyed it." Despite the turmoil that the experience had stirred up, it was humbling to be reminded that in a country where most people had what they wanted, there were so many who needed a helping hand or simply a kind gesture. Those children at the community center were a far cry from the ones for whom she planned elaborate birthday parties, kids who were raised to expect entertainment and celebrity guests and even live animals. It seemed so excessive, so wasteful.

Like her own wedding?

"Are you sticking around?" Andy asked.

Chloe checked her watch. She needed time to look for her ring before Ted arrived to pick her up for dinner. "No, I need to go."

"Okay. Well, have fun at your brunch tomorrow," he said, his voice and eyes sincere.

"Thanks," she murmured, surprised that he'd remembered.

"See you later." He gave her a little salute and walked through the busy warehouse.

Chloe drove home, feeling restless and bewildered by her reaction to Andy and to the other folks at the community center. It felt good helping people, making them smile—without getting paid for it. Andy's easygoing attitude made him a perfect fit for his truck-driving job. She wondered about his background, but then reminded herself that Andy Shearer's upbringing was none of her concern. She had so many other things on her plate to deal with.

At her apartment, she stood in the doorway of her bedroom and set her jaw. Her engagement ring had to be in this room somewhere. She began to systematically check every square inch, moving clutter and shifting furniture, covering the same ground she'd covered before, with the same result. As the time for her date with Ted drew closer, her anxiety ratcheted higher. When the doorbell rang, her mind whirled for a solution.

From a drawer she removed a flexible cast that fit like a fingerless glove. She'd needed it the time she'd sprained her wrist. Now she slid it onto her left hand and went to answer the door, worried that she might feel different about Ted in the wake of her unwelcome attraction to Andy.

But when she swung open the door and Ted stood

there holding a dozen roses, her heart grew buoyant once again.

This thing with Andy was as fleeting as her stint with Windfall. She had a wedding dress to find.

CHAPTER
∽SIX∽

"CHLOE, I KNOW it's a lot to ask," Terri said Monday morning, "but our annual golf tournament, our biggest fund-raiser of the year, is coming up later this week, and I wondered if you would mind helping there versus here in the office."

Chloe hesitated. She needed to be near the warehouse, looking for her dress, not off-site working a golf tournament. But Terri had been so kind, and Chloe had begun to feel worse about her deception....

"When is it?"

"Friday. But you wouldn't have to be there all day. Morning, afternoon, any time that you have."

"I have an event that morning, but I could get there for the afternoon. What would I be doing?"

"Directing people, taking tickets, that kind of

thing." Terri smiled. "It's more fun than hanging out here in the office."

"Okay, sure," she said, nodding. "I wouldn't mind doing something different." Besides, she intended to find her dress between now and then anyway. "As a matter of fact, I was wondering if I could help out in the warehouse this week, just for a change of pace."

Terri shrugged. "I don't mind, but it might not be good for your hand."

Chloe guiltily rubbed the elastic cast she was still wearing. "It'll be fine."

The weekend with Ted and yesterday's shower brunch had been a success, reminding her of all the reasons she was marrying him, all the reasons she was planning a big ceremony. People liked to celebrate important moments in their lives with extravagant parties—there was no crime in that. Andy himself had said it must be nice to make people happy, and it was. So she was looking forward to her supersize wedding; that didn't make her a bad person. But she was less than two weeks from getting married, and still missing a wedding gown. She seriously needed to get out into the warehouse and start poking around.

"I'm sure they could use an extra hand out there today," Terri said, "since a lot of volunteers are already at the golf tournament site, getting things ready." The telephone rang and she reached for it. "The receipts can wait," Terri added, eyeing the stack of paper in front of Chloe. "Anyone can tell you where to pitch in."

Chloe nodded and headed for the warehouse, nervously glancing around for Andy. To her relief, he was nowhere in sight. She asked more assistants about a wedding-dress shipment, but they shook their heads. One admitted that it was impossible to remember everything that came in. She noticed that assistants spotted each other off, changing stations as necessary, and some of them worked only part-time, so they wouldn't have knowledge of every incoming shipment. She walked quickly up and down the aisles, scanning for a glimpse of white, feeling a little desperate.

"I could use a hand over here," someone yelled, and Chloe turned to help. An enormous box of travel-size toiletries donated by a hotel sat on a pallet. A sturdy woman gestured to the box. "A shelter is receiving an influx of refugees this afternoon and they need sets of toiletries individually bagged to pass out."

"How many?" Chloe asked.

"As many as we can give them."

Chloe reached for a bag and began filling it with one of each kind of toiletry. Her two hours evaporated, but there was still so much more to be done that she stayed an extra hour. All the time she kept looking over her shoulder for Andy. It wasn't as if she missed him or anything; she was just so accustomed to seeing him around. But he must have had pickups or deliveries to make.

When she left to keep an appointment with a caterer to taste test sushi for an upcoming luncheon, she felt good about all the toiletries she'd bundled, but realized another morning had expired and she was no closer to finding her dress.

And so it went all week. Every morning she began looking for her gown and was pulled away by something that needed immediate attention. By Friday she still had no dress and no engagement ring. At her apartment she had resorted to emptying her bedroom of everything she could move. Only the large pieces of furniture remained, and she was considering renting a metal detector.

And strangely, she hadn't seen Andy all week. She mentioned his absence to Terri in passing, but when the woman seemed interested in why she'd noticed, Chloe changed the subject.

On the drive to the golf tournament Friday afternoon, she felt panic licking at her. She was getting married a week from tomorrow and she still hadn't found her dress, not to mention her ring. So why was she wasting her time volunteering at a fund-raising event when she should be back at the warehouse, digging through mountains of sweaters? Tomorrow she had three birthday parties back-to-back, so going to Windfall over the weekend was out of the question.

She sighed and came to a decision: on Monday she would come clean with Terri and ask for her help. And once she had her dress, she would leave with her tail between her legs.

When she found Terri at the entrance to the golf course, she considered telling her the truth and getting it over with. Dread billowed inside her.

"Thank you for coming!" Terri said, giving her a hug that made the words she'd been contemplating stick in her throat. The woman's cheeks were pink with sun and excitement. "The weather is perfect, lucky us. We need someone at the seventeenth tee to collect money for the hole-in-one contest. Are you up for it?"

"Sure," Chloe said, glad for the diversion. Monday would come soon enough. She didn't want to do anything to spoil the mood or the day.

Terri handed her a map and a blue sun visor imprinted with the Windfall logo, then pointed her in the right direction.

It was a beautiful spring day, sunny with a nip in the air. The golf course itself was lovely and green, dotted with mature trees and manicured bushes. As she walked through the crowds, inhaling the sun-scented air, she began to relax. People had come out for a good cause and spirits were high. From the turnout she surmised that the event was well established, and although things looked to be running smoothly, the event planner in her made mental notes on small details that could be improved upon.

Not that she would be around next year to offer input.

She noted signs for corporate sponsors at each of the tees and silently vowed to patronize the companies whenever possible. When she approached the seventeenth tee, there were additional signs for the hole-in-one contest. On this par-three hole, golfers paid five dollars for the chance to hit their ball into the cup in one shot. If they made a hole-in-one, an electronics company called One World would give the winner ten thousand dollars on the spot.

Chloe stepped up to another Windfall volunteer who was taking money and asked how she could help. It was a popular event, so she was instantly busy, handling cash and passing out forms. Less than an hour later a commotion arose on the tee, followed by cheers and high fives and backslapping.

"Oh, my goodness," said the woman Chloe was helping. "Somebody won!"

The crowd buzzed with excitement as walkie-talkies emerged and greensmen appeared to be verifying the shot. When a thumbs-up was given, the gallery erupted again and the man who'd made the hole-in-one gave a victory dance. From the sidelines a tall man in a sport coat and slacks emerged, grinning and holding an oversize check for ten thousand dollars. Something about him…

Chloe squinted. *Andy?*

She continued clapping and leaned over to the other volunteer. "Is that Andy Shearer?"

The woman nodded. "He owns One World Electronics. He's one of Windfall's biggest supporters. Rich, handsome *and* good-hearted…. I'd like to know what a girl would have to do to catch *his* eye."

Wonder curled through Chloe's chest. So Andy was the owner of a hugely successful company and he moonlighted as a truck driver for Windfall in his free time? He'd never even hinted that he was more than he appeared.

But then again, she'd never asked.

She was still clapping when Andy looked up and caught her gaze. He seemed surprised to see her, then gave her a nod and turned back to shake the hand of the winner and to pose for photographs.

Chloe tried not to watch him, tried to get her mind back on the task at hand. In the wake of a winner, players flooded to the tee to take their chance at the big money. Chloe took cash and handed out forms as fast as she could. Yet she was aware of Andy walking around the tee, giving encouraging pats, gesturing to other oversize checks waiting in the wings to be passed out to future winners.

And then he was making his way toward her.

Her heart beat wildly as he approached. She took money from the last people in her line and thanked them. The sight of Andy in business attire restricted her breathing, and the smile she was preparing felt shaky when he stopped in front of her.

"I didn't expect to see you here," he said.

"You're full of surprises yourself," she said, gesturing to his clothing.

He grinned. "I would've told you about One World sooner if I thought it would've made a difference."

Chloe squirmed. It wouldn't have…would it? Was she that materialistic? "How did you begin driving a truck for Windfall?"

He shrugged those big shoulders. "There was a time when I drove my own delivery truck for my business. Once my company reached a certain level of success, I felt strongly about giving back to the community. When I heard that Windfall needed trucks, I gave them one and volunteered to drive it in my spare time. Then it just became a habit."

"I'm impressed," she said, and meant it.

His blue eyes danced. "Enough to let me buy you a hot dog?"

Chloe hesitated, tempted.

"It's for a good cause," he cajoled.

She smiled and relented, telling herself it was only a concession snack, not a date.

But the hot dog lunch turned into a relaxed afternoon of strolling around the golf course, cheering on the players and pitching in wherever they were needed. Chloe asked about his business and he shared a few highlights, although she sensed he was holding back, uncomfortable with what might seem like bragging. She felt drawn to him, like those children at the community center who recognized warmth and sincerity. It was a goodness that she wanted for herself, yet she didn't think her heart was that big. When she thought of why she had volunteered for Windfall, she burned with shame.

Dusk was settling in when he walked her back to her van. Apprehensive about her burgeoning attraction to this man, Chloe pulled out her keys, ready to vault into the driver's seat.

"Did you hurt your hand?" he asked, pointing to the flexible cast.

"Er, it's just a sprain." What was another lie?

He nodded, his eyes alight with amusement. "If I were your fiancé, I might be nervous if you weren't wearing your ring—what? A week before the wedding."

"A week from tomorrow." Chloe fidgeted and looked away. "It's not what you think."

He put his hand under her chin and lifted her face until she met his gaze. "I think I'd like to kiss you right now," he said.

Chloe labored to breathe as his lips closed in on hers. "I don't… I shouldn't…"

But she did. She opened her mouth to meet his and moaned softly as they came together. His tongue gently probed hers and she responded in kind as thrilling sensations flooded her body. She wanted the fervent kiss to go on and on, but when his hand brushed her lower back, reason returned with a crash.

Chloe pulled away abruptly, covering her mouth. "I can't do this."

"You can if you want to," he said, his eyes hooded. "Chloe, I feel something between us… Something special."

She shook her head. "No. I'm not the person you think I am."

"You're beautiful and smart and kind—"

"I'm not kind," she blurted, flailing her arms. "The only reason I volunteered at Windfall was to find my lost wedding gown."

He frowned. "What?"

"My fiancé…called off the wedding and I returned my wedding gown to the bridal shop. Then we got back together and when I went to get the dress—"

"It had been donated to Windfall," he said, his voice thick.

She nodded miserably.

"The bridal shop on Queen Street?"

She nodded again.

One side of his mouth quirked back in a wry smile. "I made that pickup myself." He looked up as if searching for answers, then back to her. "So you went undercover as a volunteer just to find this dress?"

"I was desperate."

"It must be some dress."

"It's the wedding gown I've dreamed of since I was a little girl. I have to get it back."

"It's that important to you?" He gave a little laugh and jammed his hands on his hips. "This one beats everything I've ever heard or seen."

"I'm sorry," she whispered. "I didn't think anyone would get hurt."

Andy pressed his lips together as if he sorely regretted the kiss. "Don't worry. The rest of us will be fine, Chloe." Then he turned and strode away from her.

Chloe blinked back tears. It was a horrible realization for a person to learn the depths of her own selfishness. And worse—she didn't think she could change.

CHAPTER
~SEVEN~

CHLOE COULDN'T REMEMBER a more wretched weekend. How ironic that of all the Windfall drivers, Andy had been the person to collect her dress…on the day she'd noticed him in traffic with the flat tire.

The look on his face when she'd told him the truth about the gown haunted her, and the words he'd said kept playing in her head.

The rest of us will be fine, Chloe.

In other words, of everyone affected by her selfish actions, she was the person who would suffer the most.

And the kiss…

The kiss that they'd shared had been burned into her brain and onto her lips. Forgotten nuances came to her at unguarded moments—the woodsy scent of his aftershave in her lungs, the scrape of his five-o'clock shadow against her cheek, the slide of his tongue over hers.

And to make the weekend exponentially worse, a thorough search of her bedroom had not turned up her engagement ring. She'd spent hours on her knees, combing through the carpet, searching her bed linens, the floor vents, even the hem of her curtains. She knew that Ted had the ring insured, but she dreaded telling him that she'd lost a ring that had cost more than her van. In her bedroom. It didn't make sense, which only made her more crazy.

And when she woke up Monday morning, she conceded glumly that time was running out on both the ring and the dress.

She drove to Windfall with a white-knuckled grip on the steering wheel. Terri was a wonderful person who had shown her nothing but kindness, and deserved to hear the truth from her, even if Andy had already informed her of Chloe's deception.

When she arrived, she remembered the trepidation she'd felt that first morning, how she had convinced herself that donating her time to the organization somehow made up for the fact that she was volunteering under false pretenses.

But it didn't.

With her heart in her throat, she dragged herself out of the van and into the office.

Terri looked up with her usual friendly smile. "Good morning!"

"Good morning," Chloe managed to reply, fidgeting as she did so. "Terri, I came by to say that I won't be able to come in this week."

"That's okay, but you didn't have to stop by. You could've just called."

"Actually—"

"Chloe."

She looked up and blanched to see Andy standing in the door leading to the warehouse. His face was less animated than usual, but friendly nonetheless. "Can I see you for a minute?"

She fought the urge to turn and flee, but nodded and made her heavy feet move toward him.

She stepped out into the din of the warehouse, which was already buzzing with activity, voices raised in camaraderie. After the door closed behind them, she tentatively met Andy's gaze, her pulse clicking away. "Yes?"

He tore off a sheet of paper from a small notepad he held. "I tracked down that shipment I picked up from the bridal shop on Queen. The dresses were all delivered Saturday to the Helping Hand shelter— it houses families after natural disasters. They've been busy lately with all the flooding north of here. If you hurry, you can probably be there when they open. Ask for Joanie. She'll help you find what you're looking for."

Deeply touched, Chloe took the paper with a shaking hand. "I don't know how to thank you, Andy."

He gave her a rueful smile. "You can thank me by having a happy life." Then he angled his head toward Terri in the office. "She doesn't need to know about any of this."

Chloe nodded gratefully and watched him walk away for the last time.

Swallowing a lump of emotion, she returned to the office and manufactured a smile. "I was saying that I won't be able to come in this week because I'm getting married Saturday."

Terri smiled back. "Congratulations!" Then her forehead creased in a frown. "Why didn't you say something?"

Chloe shrugged. "There was just so much going on."

"That's the way it always is around here," she said with a laugh, reaching for the ringing phone. "I hope we'll see you in future, though."

Chloe nodded, but she wasn't sure she could face the people at Windfall again, knowing how she had used them.

She walked back to her van, holding the piece of notepaper in her fist. She unfolded it when she got behind the steering wheel, reading the address written in Andy's neat, masculine handwriting. What an amazing man to help her after what she'd done, and to maintain her privacy.

And right or wrong, she had to admit that she was giddy at the thought of getting her magical dress back. She was sure it would help to set her heart right again and would dispel the indefinable pangs she felt when she thought about Andy.

With traffic and a couple of missed turns, she arrived at the Helping Hand shelter about fifteen minutes after it had opened, and found it already busy. Most of the people looked sad and worried as they picked through racks, reminding Chloe once again how frivolous her quest was compared to true misfortune. She asked for Joanie, and the woman was nice enough to direct her to the small section where the formal wear hung. To her immense relief, amid the long gowns were several telltale bags from Melinda's Bridal Shop, with clear plastic windows for a glimpse of the dress inside. Chloe's heart lifted in her chest—then fell to her shoes when she saw her fairy-tale dress...

On another woman.

The young redhead stood in front of a mirror, beaming at her reflection. The magical gown fit her like a dream, sparkling and shimmering like a mirage. Chloe met her gaze in the mirror, swallowed her own bitter disappointment and smiled.

"You look beautiful," she declared.

The young woman blushed and smiled in return. "Isn't it the most magnificent dress you've ever seen?"

Chloe nodded and stepped forward. "Let me help you with the zipper."

"It seems to be stuck."

"I've got it," she said, working the zipper past the rough spot she'd created when she'd ripped off the dress in anger. "There."

"Thank you," the woman said, her voice full of wonder.

"Are you getting married?" Chloe asked.

The redhead nodded shyly. "In just a couple of weeks. But my parents' house was flooded and my dress was ruined, along with practically everything else we owned." Her eyes glistened with tears. "This gown is so much more beautiful, though. I love my David so much, and I know this dress will be a blessing on our marriage."

Chloe swallowed hard and nodded. Then she reached into the dress bag. "Look, a veil—and shoes, too. Can you wear a size seven?"

The woman nodded excitedly.

Chloe opened the box and removed the first crystal-studded silk mule and handed it to the young woman.

"Oh, my," she breathed.

"Yes, they're gorgeous," Chloe said, caressing the mate. Something rolled out of the shoe into her hand, and when she looked down, she gasped. Her engagement ring winked back at her.

Luckily, the girl hadn't noticed, so Chloe slipped the ring into her pocket, then handed over the other shoe. "You're going to be a lovely bride."

"Thank you," the young woman said, her face aglow. "I can't wait to be married."

And it hit Chloe—she didn't feel the same way about Ted as this woman did about the man she was going to marry.

Reluctantly, and with no small amount of shame, she admitted to herself that she was more excited about the wedding than about being married to Ted.

Her heart didn't flutter when he walked into a room, not the way it did when Andy was around. Ted said he loved her, but he wasn't affectionate toward her. He didn't tease her and tell her she had a great smile, or make her feel as if he'd rather eat a hot dog with her than do anything else.

"Are you okay?" the other woman asked with a little frown.

Chloe nodded. "I will be. Good luck to you."

She returned to the van and sat looking at her engagement ring with a bittersweet pang. She was infinitely relieved to have found the ring. It would be easier to tell Ted she couldn't marry him now that she could actually give it back.

TED LOOKED INCREDULOUS. "What?"

"I can't marry you," Chloe repeated, then placed the engagement ring in his hand.

"If this is some kind of payback for me breaking off the wedding earlier—"

"It isn't," she said. "In fact, I want to thank you, because your hesitation was a symptom of something that we both should have paid attention to."

"But we're good together," he protested.

"That's the problem," Chloe said. "Neither one of us should settle for 'good.' Personally, I want 'great,' and I think you do, too."

His face flushed in a way that told her he'd been having the same thoughts. From the recesses of her brain came a question about the timing of his apology—after Mindy Shale's bridal shower. She'd noticed the chemistry between them, but Ted had denied any interest in his sister's friend. Chloe closed her eyes briefly. Why did love have to be so complicated? If his sudden bout of cold feet was indeed an indication of his feelings for Mindy, she dearly hoped he made his move before the woman married someone else.

"Can I change your mind?" he asked hopefully.

Chloe shook her head. "I'm not blaming you, Ted. I've changed. I have a new perspective on life and what's important to me."

"There's no going back after this, Chloe."

"I know," she said softly. "I'll take care of undoing everything. I'll make sure everyone knows it wasn't your fault."

His smile was rueful, then he angled his head. "I don't know what it is, but you do seem different."

She released a pent-up breath. "I feel different…. I feel good." Except when she thought about Andy and the fact that she'd blown any chance she'd had with him.

Andy had spoken the truth—her deception had wound up hurting her more than anyone else.

CHAPTER
᭡—EIGHT—᭡

THE BLARE OF A horn jarred Andy from his musing—but did nothing to improve his sour mood. Why he should be so upset on the day that Chloe Parker married another man made no rational sense. The woman had told him from the beginning that she was engaged, had never encouraged his unexplainable attraction to her, had, in fact, avoided him at every turn.

Plus, his initial instincts that something fishy was going on had proved to be true—in the worst possible way. The fact that she'd used Windfall for her own selfish purposes was unbelievable. The only rationalization that mitigated her deceit was that she must truly love the man.

Which didn't make Andy feel warm and fuzzy inside.

He wheeled the truck into the Windfall parking lot, backing up to an available loading dock. He was glad to be volunteering today. Spending a few hours at Windfall always cured what ailed him, always made him realize that his problems were small, even luxurious, in the grand scheme of things.

When he walked into the warehouse, he greeted a fellow volunteer, then went to get a cup of coffee at the refreshment station. He tried to ignore the nagging sensation behind his breastbone. There was no use lamenting a never-was relationship with a woman he hadn't really known.

So much for those good instincts of his when it came to sizing up people.

You knew something wasn't right, his mind whispered, *but you overlooked it because you were falling for her.*

Oh, well, he thought as he took a swig of strong coffee, it wasn't meant to be.

He turned toward a group of people who were unloading a truck that had just arrived. His heart warmed to see volunteers pulling together, especially on a sunny Saturday when they could have been doing so many other things.

Then his steps slowed and he zoned in on one volunteer in particular.

Other things such as getting married.

Chloe Parker was one of the people who'd formed a human conveyer belt, passing bundles and boxes from the truck to the floor of the warehouse. Her cheeks were pink from exertion and a few strands of dark hair had come loose from the prim yellow ribbon of her ponytail. He'd never seen a more beautiful sight, and his heart lifted even though he told himself he had no reason to get his hopes up.

Andy joined the chain, hefting the heavier boxes. Chloe didn't notice him until they were finished. She was wiping her forehead with a bandanna when she caught his gaze. She looked away, but when she looked back, he was encouraged, and made his way over to her.

"Hi," he ventured.

"Hello."

Andy drew his hand over his mouth. "I thought today was the big day."

She nodded. "It was…supposed to be."

His heart took flight. "What happened?"

Chloe shook her head. "We canceled the wedding."

Andy reached for her hand and pulled her away from the group. "Didn't you find your dress?"

"I found it," she said, nodding. "But when I did, I realized that being married isn't about the perfect dress."

He smiled and squeezed her hand. "It isn't?"

"No," she said, squeezing back. "It's about the perfect groom."

Oblivious and uncaring of their growing audience, Andy took her into his arms. "How can I feel this way about you when we hardly know each other?"

"I don't know," she murmured, her eyes smiling. "But I feel the same way."

Happiness flooded his chest. "So...how do we go about getting to know each other?"

She thought for a few seconds, then brightened. "How do you feel about Hawaii?"

The planned honeymoon, he realized. "Hawaii sounds amazing."

Then Chloe's expression sobered. "Thank you, Andy."

"For what?"

"For reminding me what's important, for teaching me about this wonderful organization and for showing by example."

He grinned. "Does that mean I'll be seeing more of you here, too?"

She looped her arms around his neck. "Absolutely. In fact, you'll probably be heartily sick of me."

"Never," he murmured, then lowered his mouth to hers for a searing kiss.

Cheers and applause surrounded them. When they looked up, everyone was smiling and clapping with approval.

"Life is good," Chloe said in his ear.

And he agreed.

* * * * *

Dear Reader,

I can't tell you how delighted I am to be part of this edition of the *More Than Words* collection. I'm touched by Harlequin's efforts to recognize and reward organizations that make a difference in this world every single day by touching people's lives.

I have to confess, however, that when I was asked to participate by writing a novella inspired by the amazing work of Windfall Basics in Toronto, I was concerned that my humorous writing style might downplay the seriousness of their achievements. In short, I didn't want to make light of the far-reaching work of the founders, Joan Clayton and Ina Andre, or the volunteers. But editor Marsha Zinberg put my fears to rest—she trusted me to put an amusing spin on a story that would highlight the smart, compassionate work of Windfall. I hope you agree! I had so much fun writing the story of Chloe Parker, imminent bride-to-be on the hunt for a misplaced fairy-tale wedding gown, as she discovers that "It's Not About the Dress."

Most of us, me included, take so many things for granted. I can honestly say my life has been enriched after researching and writing about Windfall. My thanks to Joan and Ina and the volunteers at Windfall for creating a legacy of personal commitment. My thanks to Marsha Zinberg for inviting me to be a part of this charitable collaboration. And my thanks to you, the reader, for supporting our collective efforts to improve the lives of others…one volume of *More Than Words* at a time! Please remember this title when you purchase gifts for friends. And don't forget to visit www.windfallbasics.com for ideas on how you can help! Together, we can make a difference.

Much love and laughter,
Stephanie Bond

RONI LOMELI

∽—Shoes That Fit—∽

Looking at them, no one would guess that a little pair of girls' pink plastic jelly shoes would hold a history so touching it would be enough to break even the staunchest heart. But this pair, now sitting in an office in Claremont, California, once belonged to a little boy who was too ashamed to wear them, too embarrassed by his family's abject poverty to go to school.

Instead, he was found hiding in the bushes wearing his sister's inappropriate hand-me-down footwear.

Today the shoes belong to Roni Lomeli, executive director of Shoes That Fit, a successful charitable organization that builds the self-esteem of children in need by providing them with new shoes for school. Roni holds on to the jelly shoes as a poignant reminder of all the children she comes across in her work—and how much more work needs to be done.

But why shoes? Isn't it more important to give struggling children and their families other means of support first? In fact, shoes are vitally important when it comes to giving children a leg up at school and at home.

"When kids' shoes are torn, worn and wet, they just can't focus on their studies. They focus more on how uncomfortable they are or how often they're being teased," says Roni. "Shoes are a very important part of a child's self-esteem."

Shoes That Fit has been helping children into new footwear and clothing so they can attend school in comfort and dignity since it began in 1992. The organization's story started with another little boy at a school in Pomona, California, found crying on the playground and saying his feet hurt.

When the school nurse examined him, she pulled off his shoes and discovered that his parents had curled his toes under and stuffed his little feet into shoes at least three sizes too small. The nurse rubbed his feet, stuffed them back into the shoes and sent him on his way. When she was asked why she didn't do more, she responded, "We have so many kids like this, I don't know where to start."

Something had to be done.

That "something" turned into Shoes That Fit. Today, despite operating without any government funding—all money comes from private and corporate donations—Shoes That Fit has gone from helping one school in one state to helping over one thousand seven hundred schools in forty-two states across the U.S. In 2012 alone, it gave out an astounding one hundred sixteen thousand items.

Stepping up to the plate

Roni has been with the charity since nearly the beginning. In 1993, when her oldest daughter started kindergarten, she responded to a note from the principal's office asking for help to find kids' footwear for children in a neighboring community. She wrote back and said she would do it.

In the early years Roni, who was also working as an insurance executive, followed the charity's program: she would help a nearby school identify children in need, the school would measure their feet, she would write down the measurements and post them on cards then she'd put them on a bulletin board at her daughter's private school. Teachers and parents could take a card, go to a store and buy the corresponding pair of shoes, and Roni would drop them off.

This traditional model still works today, with hundreds of volunteers from schools, churches, businesses and civic organizations across the country pitching in.

Yet although she liked her work in insurance back then, she soon found herself more and more involved in Shoes That Fit.

"I was probably there every day! I've seen all angles and I've done all angles," she says of her eventual climb from volunteer to executive director in

2001 when the founder retired. Roni admits she was nervous making the leap to the nonprofit sector, since she had two girls preparing for college by that time, but her husband was behind her 100 percent.

What hasn't changed over the years is the compassionate spirit in which the shoes are given.

No one wants the stigma of being a child "in need," so Roni ensures that all donations are given in private. The kids are simply asked to leave their class early at the end of the day and receive their new shoes away from the prying eyes of others. The next morning they're ready for school in a new pair of comfy shoes, just like all the other students in their classes.

The Shoes That Fit staff and volunteers provide new athletic shoes that are attractive and comfortable. Brand names are great, but flashy shoes are out. Shoes should have simple styling that will appeal to the widest range of children, says Roni.

All this work and attention to detail pays off.

"When the kids get their shoes, they skip. They're so excited," says Roni. "They want to keep their boxes. But you know, it's sad. Many have never had a shoe box before."

The joy of giving back

Not surprisingly, letters from teachers, parents and students pour in each year.

"I just wanted you to know what joy it brings to me to see the look in the children's eyes when I tell them someone cared enough to get them shoes that fit. We have many children who come to us while living in a shelter. New shoes, underwear and socks give them a chance at making friends and coping with what is happening in their lives," wrote one school nurse.

Or as a little boy, Eduardo, put it so succinctly, "I like my new shoes. They feel so good when I walk in them. I am happy. Thank you."

Letters like these keep Roni going. So does all the support she receives from her daughters, Lacey and Emily, who still help out at Shoes That Fit each week. Roni says one of the things she's most proud of is how her work at the nonprofit has shaped her own children's sense of volunteerism.

"My girls are very, very compassionate. It's important as parents to pass that on to our kids so they can pass it on to theirs and this can keep going," she says.

While successes mount each day, Roni says the next goal is to partner with more corporations and cover other states to reach out to as many children as possible, particularly as the economy staggers and more families need help.

It's imperative that Shoes That Fit keep moving forward, because for every child forced to wear pink jelly shoes or shoes much too small for comfort, there is a solution.

"We hear the sad stories, but at the same time, we can take those stories and make them better for somebody," Roni says. "People think they have a calling…and I think this was mine."

For more information, visit www.shoesthatfit.org, or write to Shoes That Fit, 1420 N. Claremont Blvd., Suite 204A, Claremont, CA 91711.

MAUREEN CHILD

⌖THE PRINCESS SHOES⌖

⊱—MAUREEN CHILD—⊰

USA TODAY bestselling author Maureen Child is a native Californian now living in the mountains of Utah. Experiencing a change of season for the first time is exciting, but living with snow is quite the adventure! As the author of more than one hundred books, Maureen loves a happy ending and still swears that she has the best job in the world. When she isn't writing, she's reading or traveling with her husband.

Visit Maureen's website, at www.maureen-child.com, or her Facebook page.

CHAPTER
ONE

"I'LL HAVE MY assistant fax you the numbers this afternoon." Noah Fielding smiled into the phone and mentally congratulated himself on the deal he'd just struck.

In one month he would be adding another shopping mall, this one in Seal Beach, California, to his list of holdings. Which would bring the total so far to six. And this was merely the beginning. He'd spent a lifetime building his plans and now, seeing them all come to fruition was… *Satisfying* was the wrong word. Perhaps *anticlimactic* was the right one.

Frowning, he nodded as the man on the other end of the line continued to talk, but Noah was already distancing himself from the conversation. Deal was done. End of business. Finally he interrupted. "Fine, Matt. Once your people draw up the contracts, I'll have my lawyers go over them and I'm sure everything will be settled."

Another minute or two and he hung up, thinking that he should be happier about all of this. Ten years ago he'd started on his empire by buying up a dying mall in Crescent Bay, California, and putting his own stamp on it. Now that shopping center—Fielding Center Mall, his headquarters—was a small, but thriving, center on the coast between Orange County and San Diego. He'd tapped in to exactly what people wanted—small-town feel, big-city wares. And because of his success here, he'd been able to expand far faster than he'd expected.

And still something was missing.

Which was irritating in the extreme.

Still scowling, he stood and paced the confines of his office. He couldn't put his finger on what was wrong, but the feeling remained, like an uncomfortable itch at the back of his neck. He stopped in front of the window opening into his assistant's office and peered between the partially opened blinds at Annie Moore.

Six months she'd been working for him, and in that time he'd found her efficient, friendly and all too distracting. She was tall, with short blond hair, pale blue eyes and a figure he shouldn't even be noticing.

"Never should have hired a beautiful woman," he muttered as he watched her fingers fly over her keyboard. But then, he hadn't hired her because of her looks or even her office skills, though they were impressive. No, he'd offered her a job because she was a single mother and he recognized worry when he saw it. She'd come to him looking to make a fresh start for herself and her daughter. And she'd clearly been anxious about finding a job that would pay for the kind of life she wanted to give her child.

That Noah understood. And respected.

It was merely coincidence that his own dissatisfaction with his life had become noticeable at the same time she'd started working for him.

Then the outer office door opened, one of his security guards walked in escorting Annie's young daughter, and Noah's thoughts scattered. The girl was crying and Carlos looked grim. Noah's curiosity got the better of him. Quietly he partially opened his office door.

"Ms. Moore," a deep voice announced, "I think we have a problem."

Problems were nothing new to Annie Moore. She was the first line of defense at the Fielding Center Mall in Crescent Bay. As Noah Fielding's executive assistant, Annie had been called on to unravel dilemmas and resolve crises almost daily since she first got the job six months before. Still, she'd been hoping for a respite so she could finish typing up Noah's correspondence and clear off her desk early for a change.

No such luck.

She turned from her computer monitor to glance at the doorway where Carlos Miranda, one of the mall security guards, stood, one hand on the shoulder of Annie's six-year-old daughter, Kara.

Fear settled in the pit of her stomach. Tears were still tracking down Kara's cheeks and Carlos looked troubled. Annie jumped up and came around her desk, throwing a quick, uneasy glance at her boss's door.

One of the perks of her job was being able to bring her daughter to the office after school. Kara didn't have to go into day care and Annie didn't have to worry about her little girl's safety. At least she never had before. Now, though, the fear inside her was making her stomach jitter as if it held a thousand bees flying in formation.

"Kara, honey," Annie whispered, going down on one knee in front of her daughter. Automatically she ran her hands up and down Kara's arms and legs, as if making sure she was all in one piece. When she was satisfied for the moment, she asked, "What is it? What happened? Are you all right?"

"She's fine," Carlos assured her in a deep, rumbling voice. "Just a little scared."

"Scared?" Annie's mind picked up on that one word and ran with it. Just half an hour ago she'd given Kara permission to go to the cookie shop for an after-school snack, with instructions to come right back. It was a small-town shopping center. Everyone in the mall knew Kara and looked out for her, so Annie had thought her daughter was safe. Clearly she'd been wrong. Obviously she was a terrible mother. She never should have allowed Kara to go off alone. "Scared of what, baby?" she asked, almost afraid to hear. "What happened?"

"Mommy, I'm really sorry."

Kara's tears erupted then and her small body shook with the force of her sobs. She threw herself into her mom's arms and as Annie held her, nearly frantic now, she looked up at Carlos, her mind dredging up all sorts of horrible things and hoping to heaven she was wrong about all of them. "What's going on? You said she was all right. Was she hurt?"

"Kara's fine," he said, reassuring her even as worry of a different sort began to mount.

If she hadn't been hurt, then why all the tears?

Carlos clasped his hands in front of him, looking as though he were a soldier standing at parade rest. His gray-streaked black hair was cut short, and though his mouth was firm and tight, his dark brown eyes were soft as he looked at her. "I'm afraid we're going to have to talk to Mr. Fielding. The owner of the shoe store, Mrs. Higgins, called my office. It seems Kara was caught shoplifting."

Kara cried even louder and seemed to shrink into herself.

"Shoplifting?" Shock colored Annie's voice as she set Kara back from her so that she could look into her daughter's eyes. This she hadn't expected at all. "Is that true? Were you stealing?"

The little girl's blond braids were messy from a day of playing at school. Her white blouse carried a jelly stain and her jeans had grassy marks at the knees. Her pink sneakers were scuffed and one shoe was untied. Her big blue eyes overflowed with tears again as she nodded and gulped in air.

"I didn't mean to…." she said, her words trailing off into another heart-wrenching sob.

Annie didn't even know what to say. Kara had never done anything like this before and she couldn't understand why the girl had done it now. What could possibly have motivated her to steal? "Kara, baby, you know better. Stealing is wrong."

"But—"

"No," Annie said quickly, cutting off whatever excuse Kara might have offered. "There is no 'but.' Stealing is wrong. If you want something, you have to save your allowance until you have enough to buy it."

"I couldn't wait, Mommy," she said on a rising wail of misery. "It's important."

Fear had drained away and even her initial shock was starting to fade, leaving Annie feeling mostly stunned and like a failure as a parent. She could see it all now. Her six-year-old daughter was already beginning a life of crime.

She shook her head and said, "Nothing is so important that you do something you know is wrong, Kara. If you wanted a new pair of shoes so badly, you should have come to me and asked for them."

"But the shoes aren't for me." She swiped tears away with her dirty fingers and sniffed loudly. "I was only trying to help Gracie."

Now Kara was more confused than ever. Of course, she knew Gracie O'Malley was Kara's best friend. The two little girls were inseparable, even sitting beside each other in their first-grade class. Annie had seen them together on the playground, but since she and Kara had lived in Crescent Bay only six months, there hadn't been much time to settle in and meet the families of her daughter's friends.

Clearly she should have made the time.

Frowning now, Annie asked, "Did Gracie ask you to steal something for her?"

"'Course not. She didn't even know. It was going to be a present. A surprise."

"Is it her birthday?" Annie was trying to make sense of something that made no sense.

"No…." Kara blew out a breath and rubbed her nose.

This was one of those times when Annie wished she weren't a single mother. She wished Kara's father had lived long enough to help raise their daughter, because right now she'd really appreciate a little backup.

But the truth was, Annie was on her own. And usually that was fine with her. When Kara's father died, Annie had promised herself that she wasn't going to be one of those moms who had a steady stream of "uncles" moving in and out of her daughter's life. She'd vowed to give Kara a good, steady upbringing. Which meant, for Annie, that romance wouldn't be a part of her life until Kara was at least a teenager. Not that she was besieged by offers of dates anyway. After all, single moms weren't high on the dating food chain.

Still, she'd tried to give Kara enough love and support for two parents, so that her daughter would never miss out on having a father. But at moments like these Annie wondered if she'd succeeded.

Sighing, she looked up at the security guard, realizing he was still standing there, observing all the drama. No doubt he was waiting for the hysterics to end so that he could report this to Noah Fielding. Just the thought of that made Annie pale. Her boss was a fair but cool and distant man. What would his reaction be to his assistant's daughter becoming a thief? She didn't want to think about it. If he was angry enough, he could fire Annie, and then where would they be?

No, she had to get to the bottom of this situation so that she could have as much information as possible before facing Noah. And knowing her daughter, Annie had the feeling she wouldn't be getting any answers out of Kara until they were alone. "Do we really have to bring this to Mr. Fielding right now? Couldn't I take care of this myself by speaking with Mrs. Higgins?"

"Well…" The big man hedged a bit and looked even more uncomfortable than Annie felt. After another long moment or two, though, his kind brown eyes settled on Kara briefly and he said, "All right, then. I'll tell Mrs. Higgins to expect you this afternoon."

"Thank you." When Carlos left, Annie looked at her daughter. Keeping her voice low, she said, "Now, Kara Elizabeth Moore, I want you to tell me what on earth you were doing by trying to steal those shoes for Gracie."

Kara huffed out a breath, sniffed loudly and said, "Gracie doesn't have good shoes, Mommy. Today she was wearing her big sister's and they fell off during recess and the other kids laughed at her and Gracie cried."

Fresh tears accompanied that statement and Annie's heart twisted in sympathy with her daughter's misery.

"They really hurt her feelings, Mommy, and I got mad, but they wouldn't stop laughing and—" The little girl ran out of words and flung herself into her mother's arms again.

Her sobs reverberated through Annie's body as she felt both pride and disappointment. Of course she hated that her daughter had tried to steal something, but how could she not be proud that Kara had been trying to do something wonderful for her friend?

Sometimes, she thought, being a parent was like trying to dance on a tightrope.

She'd had no idea that Gracie's family was having such a hard time of things. But Kara had known and had done what a six-year-old child felt was necessary.

Taking a deep breath, Annie plunged into suddenly deep parental waters and, like all parents everywhere, sent out a silent prayer hoping she was saying the right thing. "Honey, I'm so proud of you for wanting to help Gracie. But you really went about it the wrong way."

"But I don't have enough money," Kara wailed, burrowing closer to her mother.

"That doesn't mean it's all right to take what doesn't belong to you," Annie chided. "You should have come to me, sweetie."

All at once Kara pulled back, looked into her mom's eyes and thrust her bottom lip out. It was a stubborn expression Annie was all too familiar with. "Gracie's all embarrassed and I didn't want to tell anybody else so I thought I could fix it myself and now it got worse and Gracie still doesn't have the shoes and I'm in trouble and—"

"Baby, I know you were trying to help. But to steal something?" She shook her head. "That's wrong no matter what the reason is. Besides, Mommy works for the man who owns the mall. He's not going to be happy when he finds out about this."

"Will he be mad?"

"What's going on in here?"

A new voice entered the conversation, interrupting Kara's stream of chatter, and Annie's stomach did a quick nosedive. Noah. She supposed it was inevitable that he would have heard the commotion and come out to investigate. Nothing got past that man. He had his finger on the pulse of everything that happened in his world.

They were about to learn the answer to her daughter's last question. Annie closed her eyes briefly. What if he fired her? What would she do then? She and Kara were happy in Crescent Bay. They were settling in, making a home. What were the chances she could find another job making the same kind of salary in such a small town? And she doubted she'd find another position that allowed her to have her daughter with her after school.

As these and a million other wild thoughts raced through her mind, she muffled a sigh. Taking hold of Kara's hand, Annie stood up to face her boss.

He was tall, with broad shoulders, a square jaw and midnight-black hair. His pale blue eyes looked almost icy against his tanned skin, and the fact that he wasn't smiling didn't make Annie feel any better.

"Noah…"

Kara scuttled behind her mother as if trying to hide, and Annie really couldn't blame her. Ordinarily, Noah wasn't the warmest human being in the world. And to a child who knew she was in trouble, he probably looked even more forbidding.

"I'm sorry about this," Annie said, "but something's come up and I need to go and handle it."

He ignored her, which Annie was used to. In the time she'd worked for him, he'd made a point of maintaining a safe, polite distance between them. He was always courteous, but remote. As if he was deliberately trying to keep her at arm's length.

So it was a complete surprise when he came forward until he was standing right beside her. With a stern look on his face, he looked down at Kara and asked, "Were you stealing?"

Annie groaned inwardly.

Kara clutched at her mom's black slacks and looked up at Noah. "Uh-huh. But I'm really sorry."

"Do you know why you're sorry?" he asked, his voice quiet, deep.

Annie didn't know what to do. She felt as though she should step in, but at the same time, he was her boss, the owner of the mall, and at the moment he was handling Kara so gently that she found herself simply observing. There was no anger in his tone, no impatience, and Annie was relieved by it.

"'Cause it's wrong to take stuff that isn't yours," the little girl answered.

Annie smoothed her hand over Kara's soft blond hair and then lifted her gaze to Noah. He looked directly at her and seemed to be waiting for her to say something. "Kara made a mistake and she's very sorry. She's going to apologize to Mrs. Higgins, too. Aren't you, sweetie?"

Kara sighed. "Yes, Mommy."

Smiling now, Annie put on a brave face and didn't let any of her thoughts show.

"I'm sorry about this, too, Noah," Annie said quickly. "It's never happened before and I promise you it won't happen again."

He only nodded, then looked to Kara again. "Do you still want the shoes?"

"Uh-huh, but I don't have money."

Tucking his hands into the pockets of his slacks, Noah simply stood there, staring down at the little girl for a long moment. His features were impossible to read, so Annie felt a jolt of surprise when he spoke again.

"Would you like the chance to earn the money?"

Apparently her daughter was as surprised as she was. Kara let go of Annie's pants and moved out from behind her. Still sniffling, the girl tipped her head back to look up at him. "I'm just a little girl. I don't have a job."

His lips curved slightly. "Even children can earn the things they want. I'll pay you five dollars a day to do chores here around the office. Then you can save your money and buy your friend the new shoes."

Annie was stunned speechless.

Kara, on the other hand, was not. "You mean it?"

"I do." Then he looked at Annie. "If it's all right with your mother."

Annie met his steady blue eyes and found herself nodding agreement. She hadn't expected this from her usually taciturn employer. Not only was he being kind, but he had given Kara the opportunity to work for something she wanted.

When he smiled, something inside Annie seemed to wake up and start humming. Who would have guessed that Noah Fielding had a heart?

CHAPTER
∽TWO∽

TWO HOURS LATER Noah was still just as surprised at his actions as Annie. It had been years since he'd done anything spur-of-the-moment, and he wasn't exactly known for being an altruistic kind of guy. Still, the crestfallen expression on the little girl's face had tugged at his long-neglected heart. But it was more than just the child. More than watching Annie comfort her daughter. He'd unexpectedly found himself remembering his own past—a past that he preferred to keep locked away.

Noah Fielding didn't look backward. He always had his eye on the future because the years behind him meant nothing. They didn't define who he was now. And the boy he'd once been had been neatly supplanted by the man he'd become. Drive, determination and ambition had locked the door on a past that he preferred never to think about.

But Kara's tears had tugged at him so that he hadn't been able to turn his back. Now he was wondering just what the hell he'd been thinking. Getting involved with Annie and her daughter was a mistake on so many levels he could hardly count them all. In one fell swoop he'd knocked down the wall of deliberate formality he'd created between him and his assistant.

During the time Annie had been working for him, he'd managed to consistently ignore her presence, beyond her talent for efficiency. Now that they'd each breached that businesslike facade, though, there would be no going back. It wasn't easy to put the proverbial cat back into the bag. By stepping into the situation, Noah had made it far more complex.

The Moore females were clearly a dangerous duo.

"You've dug yourself a hole now," he muttered and took a seat behind his desk. Trying to put Annie and her daughter out of his mind—at least for the moment—he dived back into work.

"I'M REALLY SORRY," Kara said, staring up at Mrs. Higgins, the owner of the franchised discount shoe store. "I won't ever do it again, either. I promise."

Thankfully, the shop was empty at the moment, giving Kara the opportunity to apologize in private for what she'd done. Annie was as nervous about this as her daughter, so she was grateful they didn't have an audience.

People out in the enclosed mall wandered past the store, unaware of the little drama going on inside.

The shop itself had long aisles stuffed with opened shoe boxes for customers to browse through, and did a booming business in children's shoes. Annie had been in many times, both for her daughter and herself. So Mrs. Higgins was not only familiar, she was practically a friend, which only added to the misery of the moment.

Mrs. Higgins's kind brown eyes were filled with understanding as she looked down at Kara. "I'm glad to hear you're sorry, Kara. I have to say I was very disappointed in you."

Annie took a breath and inwardly cringed. "Kara knows she was wrong to do what she did and she's going to make up for it, aren't you?"

The little girl dipped her head, swiped the toe of her tennis shoe against the gray carpet and murmured, "Yes, ma'am."

"I want to thank you for being so understanding about this," Annie said.

"Nonsense. Every child makes mistakes. It's how they learn. But Kara, I'd like to know why you wanted those shoes so badly." Mrs. Higgins looked down at the little girl's pink sneakers. "You're wearing a pair just like the ones you took."

"They're for my friend Gracie, because she doesn't have any."

"I see."

"But now I have a job and I'm going to buy those shoes for Gracie really soon."

"Is that so? Well, now, that's a nice thing to do for your friend. So I'll tell you what." Mrs. Higgins walked over to a nearby shelf, took down the box of shoes that Kara had tried to steal and put them behind her counter. "I'll just hold on to them for you, so they'll be here waiting for you when you have the money to buy them, all right?"

Kara grinned and practically bounced on her heels, already recovered from the humiliation of an apology. "Thank you! I'll have the money soon, because I'm a hard worker, Mommy says."

"Good for you."

Annie gave Kara's hand a squeeze and said, "Sweetie, go wait for me by the door, all right?"

The little girl skipped away, and when she was out of earshot, Annie turned back to Mrs. Higgins. "Honestly, I don't even know what to say to you. Thank you so much for being so kind."

The older woman shook her head and let her gaze slide to where Kara waited, watching the people in the mall walk by. "She's a good girl and she's sorry. So that's taken care of. What I worry about is the reason Kara was stealing."

"For her friend, you mean."

Nodding, Mrs. Higgins met Annie's eyes. "You know, some families around here aren't doing well at all. And the children are the ones who end up losing. Owning a shoe store, you see the kids come in, wearing shoes that are worn-out or don't fit, and you wonder if there isn't something you could be doing to help." She frowned and gave a small sigh. "Your Kara—even though she went about it the wrong way—was at least trying to do something about the situation. You've got a loving little girl there, Annie. You should treasure her."

"I do," she said, turning to look at her daughter, safe and happy and well fed. With Mrs. Higgins's words ringing in her ears, she couldn't help thinking about what it would be like not to be able to provide something as simple as shoes for your child.

When someone walked through the door, setting off a chime of welcome, Annie excused herself, and the older woman hustled off to serve her customer. She and Kara strolled through the mall, and Annie took her time going back to the office. As well as this had all turned out, she was still concerned not only by what Mrs. Higgins had said, but by her daughter's brief foray into shoplifting.

After leading Kara to a white bench beside a gurgling fountain, Annie sat down and looked at the little girl.

"Why now?" she asked after a long moment of silence broken by the sound of her daughter's heels kicking the railing beneath the bench. "I mean, what made you decide to steal these shoes for Gracie today, sweetie? Why not last week? Or the week before?"

Kara sighed, scratched at her knee and shrugged. "Gracie used to have her own shoes, but they got too small and they were making her toes hurt. But her mommy said they couldn't get new ones right now, so she had to start wearing her sister's old ones." Shaking her head, she said, "Gracie's daddy lost his job in the city and he's worried a lot now, but it's not fair, Mommy. Gracie shouldn't have to get laughed at in school."

"No, she shouldn't," Annie agreed. Her mind turned immediately to the fact that if she didn't have this job with Noah, Kara might have been the one to be laughed at by her schoolmates. Even with a good job, money was sometimes too tight for comfort. She couldn't imagine how bad Gracie's mother must be feeling not to be able to provide her child with a good pair of shoes. And according to Mrs. Higgins, the O'Malley family wasn't the only one in town having trouble.

While Kara sat beside her, safe and happy now, Annie looked around the mall. Wide skylights spilled sunshine down on customers carrying bags of merchandise from store to store. The floor gleamed, with brick-colored Spanish tiles beneath walls painted a soft adobe peach. The merchandise for sale was widely divergent, everything from discount shoes to high-end clothing.

In this spot, the world looked prosperous, and yet there were children out there who didn't even have a pair of shoes to call their own.

Annie had been unemployed only once since Kara was born, and those few months had terrified her. She'd lain awake at night, hoping her savings would hold out until she could find another job. Praying she'd be able to take care of her little girl as she deserved to be taken care of.

She felt a swift, sharp stab of sympathy for Gracie's mom and for however many other moms were in the same position. How easy life seemed when you were working. Well, not easy, she corrected mentally. But certainly as long as you had a job, you felt somehow safer. Knew that you could find a way to take care of your family.

What must it be like for Gracie's parents? They had three children to worry over. They would have gone through any savings they might have had much faster than Annie had. Her heart ached again, not just for the little girl in the ill-fitting shoes, but for the mom and dad who were unable to change the situation.

"She's not the only one, either," Kara said softly.

"What?" Annie's gaze shot back to her daughter.

"Gracie." Kara twisted the ends of her hair around her finger and said, "Some of the other kids have worn-out shoes with big holes in them and their feet get all wet when it rains or something and…"

As Kara talked and Annie listened, she recalled what Mrs. Higgins had said, and she couldn't bear the thought that children in her community were lacking something so basic. How was it possible she hadn't even known about it? And what could she do about it? Something to definitely think about.

With her mind still whirling, she took Kara's hand and headed back to her office.

BY THE END OF THE afternoon, when Kara was busy dusting the bookshelves and equipment in her mother's office, Noah wasn't surprised when Annie knocked on his door and stepped inside.

"Before I leave for the day, I just wanted to thank you again," she said when he looked up at her.

"Not necessary." He didn't want her thanks. What he did want from her he couldn't—shouldn't—have.

"I think it is." She stepped closer to the desk, and with that single step, Noah caught a whiff of her perfume drifting toward him. "What you did for Kara was really very sweet. Very understanding."

"That's the first time anyone's ever accused me of being sweet," he admitted, leaning back in his desk chair to study her more closely.

She looked uncomfortable, but he supposed he could understand that. In the months they'd worked together, their relationship had been strictly business. Today was the first time they'd ever crossed that polite bridge separating them. And it seemed that Annie was a bit ill at ease about it. Noah knew exactly what she was feeling.

He'd been thinking about her all day. Now that he'd breached the wall between them, it was as if his mind and body had decided that all bets were off. For six months Noah had done everything he could to ignore the hum of attraction he felt for her. Not just because she was his employee, but because she was a single mom and more vulnerable than most. He might think of himself as a cold bastard, but even he had lines he didn't cross. Still, that hum was there, and now it was more noticeable than ever.

Sweet? He wasn't feeling sweet.

She laughed a little and folded her hands together, fingers twisting nervously. "Well, whether you think so or not, it was kind of you to not—"

"What?" he interrupted, reading her expression easily. "Fire you?" Noah stood up from behind his desk so that he could meet her gaze squarely. "Did you really expect that I would fire you over your daughter's mistake?"

She blew out a breath that ruffled the short fringe of bangs on her forehead. "Yeah, I thought it was a possibility."

"It wasn't."

"Some men might have."

He couldn't imagine who, but that wasn't the point. "Not me."

"Yes, I can see that now." She smiled, her blue eyes shining. "Anyway, I do appreciate it. And you were so good to Kara, offering her a job to earn money…."

He brushed that aside, since he wasn't entirely comfortable with the offer he'd made. Noah lived his life by a simple rule. Don't get involved.

Yet today he'd not only shattered that rule, he was actually having a hard time regretting the action. How had Annie and her daughter reached inside him and pulled out feelings and emotions he'd thought long buried?

"I know what it's like to be a kid and to want something so badly you'd do anything to have it—"

Noah stopped suddenly, sharply aware that he'd said more than he'd planned to.

But thankfully Annie didn't ask questions.

His past was just that. The past. He refused to spend time thinking about drifting from foster home to foster home with nothing more than a paper bag containing secondhand clothing to call his own. He remembered clearly the constant worry and the gnawing desperation, the hunger to be…more.

Which was why he'd made a vow to get through school no matter what it took. To work hard. To invest his money. To never again be susceptible to anyone else's whims. And now that he'd succeeded, he wasn't interested in remembering what had compelled him to get there.

"You're different from most people, then," she said softly. "Most of us can't remember what it was like to be a child. To know that sometimes impulses lead to bad decisions."

Truer words were never spoken, he thought. Hadn't his own impulse to help brought him to this very spot? He walked around the edge of his desk, drawn by the warmth in her eyes as much as by the scent of springtime that clung to her. She didn't back up, simply stood there as he got nearer.

Now a new and very distracting impulse was taking hold of him, he told himself, dropping his gaze to the lush curve of her mouth. He wanted to kiss her. Taste her. And that would only compound the mistake he'd already made. He wasn't interested in connections, and Annie Moore had strings wrapped all around her. So, yeah, he had an impulse, but unlike a kid, he had better control over it.

Although if she kept looking at him as she was now, he wasn't entirely sure how much control he'd be able to hold on to.

CHAPTER
~THREE~

"EVERYBODY MAKES MISTAKES." Eager to get past the urge to reach for her, he shifted the conversation away from him. "That's true."

"Your daughter's a good kid."

Instantly her face brightened. "She really is."

"How long has her father been gone?" Scowling, he cursed himself for the blunt question. He hadn't actually meant to ask it aloud. It was just that he needed to know if she was still mourning her late husband.

Some of that brightness faded as she glanced back over her shoulder at the little girl rubbing her dust cloth across the desk with more enthusiasm than precision. Turning her gaze back to Noah, she said, "My husband died when Kara was a baby."

Selfishly, he was glad to hear it. He didn't want

her still yearning for the man she'd lost. Not when she could be thinking about him.

That notion scuttled through his mind so fast, he hardly recognized it as his own. Where the hell was this coming from?

"It must have been tough on you. Both of you." His voice was low, as was hers. He told himself that he was just being nice. That none of this meant anything. But even he was beginning to doubt it.

"Sometimes," she admitted, then almost unconsciously squared her shoulders and stiffened her spine. "It's not easy being a single parent."

No, it couldn't be, he thought, though he had no way of knowing. But he did know that as a kid, he'd envied the children with parents.

"And as evidenced today," she added with a sheepish smile, "I'm not a perfect mother."

"Nobody's perfect," he assured her quickly. "Besides, all a kid really needs is to be loved. Everything else sorts itself out."

She tipped her head to one side. "Is that experience talking again?"

Okay, they were getting in far deeper than he'd intended. He hadn't meant to steer the conversation back down this path. He'd simply been anxious to keep that wall between them from rebuilding itself. Which just went to show he wasn't thinking clearly. Because the best thing for both of them would be if the wall sprang up fast, harder and stronger than it had been before.

But she was looking at him, her big blue eyes drawing him in deeper and deeper.

"No experience," he told her, deliberately misunderstanding her. "No kids."

"I didn't mean—but you were so good with Kara, I just assumed…"

"You've known me six months," he reminded her. "If I had a family, you would have seen them by now."

"Why don't you?" she whispered, then sucked in a gulp of air, shook her head and said, "Sorry. Sorry. Don't know why I asked that. It's none of my business."

"Not a big secret," he said with a shrug. "I spent the past ten years working, building my business. A wife and kids would have slowed me down."

She blinked. "Well, that's honest."

"You'll always get honest from me, Annie." But his brand of honesty wasn't the kind her type of woman wanted to hear. She wouldn't be interested in a man who didn't want to tie himself to a family. A home. And if he had any sense at all, he'd be pulling back from her right now.

"Um…"

Just do it, he told himself. Bust out of this conversation, rebuild that wall of formality and step away. His brain knew what to do, but his body was fighting him.

"I'm all finished, Mommy!"

A small voice shattered the growing tension between him and Annie, and Noah knew he should be grateful for the respite. He was attracted to her, sure, but Annie Moore and her daughter had *complications* written all over them. Complications he didn't want or need.

"That's great, honey," Annie said, turning to face her daughter as if she, too, were thankful for an excuse to tear her gaze from his. "Why don't you get your backpack and we'll head home." She checked her watch. "The bus is due in half an hour."

"I don't like the bus," Kara complained, scuffing one shoe against the floor. "It smells bad."

"Bus?" Noah leaned one hip against his desk and folded his arms over his chest.

Annie sighed. "My car's in the shop. Something about points and pistons...or something like that anyway. It'll be ready by next week. Meantime, the bus goes right by our house."

"And smells bad," Kara reminded everyone.

Why the idea of Annie and her daughter standing at a bus stop bothered him, Noah didn't know. After all, Crescent Bay was a small town, and they'd no doubt be safe enough. Still, imagining the two of them on a damned bench when he had a perfectly good car parked outside was just irritating.

"I'll take you home."

"No," Annie said, immediately shaking her head. "That's not necessary at all."

"Yay!" Kara crowed, and swung her pink backpack over her shoulder.

Odd, but it bothered him that she was willing to turn down a ride with him in favor of a public bus.

Hell, he ought to be thanking her. Instead, he said, "It's just a ride, Annie."

She looked undecided, but her daughter turned wide, pleading eyes up to her and said, "Please, Mommy? I don't like the bus."

Annie was wavering, Noah could tell. Clearly her daughter was her weak spot, and he liked that about her. A kid deserved to be her mother's focus. Even if she might be uncomfortable asking for help, she was willing to bend for her daughter's sake.

"I don't know…."

"It's not like you're out of my way," he said reasonably, silently wondering why he was trying so hard to convince her. "Crescent Bay is so small, everything is close by."

"Well…"

"That means yes!" Kara grinned up at him as if they were conspirators and had just pulled off a tricky mission. Noah found himself grinning back. Hard to resist a six-year-old heartbreaker with a gap-toothed smile.

Annie laughed shortly. "All right, then. We accept. And thank you. Again."

He looked down at her. He didn't want her gratitude. He wanted…something he shouldn't from a woman so tied to home and family. "You're going to have to stop thanking me."

"You make that difficult."

"Can we go now?" Kara wanted to know.

"Yeah. We can go. But first…" He pulled his wallet from his pocket, flipped through the bills inside and pulled out a five. "Here's your salary, young lady."

Kara took it with wide eyes, then shot her mother a victorious look. "Wow. Look, Mommy! I got paid just like you!"

"Yes, you did, baby. And you have a very under-standing boss, it seems."

Noah moved to the closet, grabbed his suit jacket and slipped it on. When he turned around to face her, he was caught up in the beauty of her smile as she looked at him. His chest felt suddenly tight and air had to force its way into his lungs. *Six months* was all he could think. Six months she'd been in his of-fice, and this was the first time he'd seen that smile of hers directed fully at him.

He wanted to see it again. Soon.

Then she spoke. "Honestly, Noah, as nice as this is, you don't really have to do it."

"Yeah," he said quietly. "I think I do."

He took her elbow and a slow rush of warmth filled him. He steered her toward the door, pausing only long enough for her to scoop her purse off the edge of her desk.

Kara hurried out of the office in front of them, her quick, light footsteps tapping like a racing heartbeat. "It's just a ride, Annie," he said again.

But even he didn't completely believe that.

OVER THE NEXT few days the atmosphere in the of-fice seemed to shift somehow. Kara had always been there after school, of course, but before the incident with the shoes, Noah had more or less ignored the girl's presence.

Now Kara was running in and out of his office with impunity, doing her "job." And Noah didn't seem to have a problem with it at all. Most men would have been irritated by Kara's constant stream of chatter. Instead, Noah was infinitely patient with the girl. Annie was frankly amazed at how well her daughter and her boss were getting along. And to think she'd believed Noah Fielding to be a cold man.

She couldn't have been more wrong. He treated Kara like a miniadult. He listened when she told him stories about school and gave her his full attention when she talked about Gracie and the princess shoes Kara was planning to buy for her friend.

He'd even insisted that Kara call him Noah, saying that Annie's direction to her daughter to call him "Mr. Fielding" was not necessary. And between the two of them, Annie had simply lost that minor battle.

Hard to argue with the growing relationship between her little girl and Noah, though. Kara was blooming under his interest. Annie hadn't even realized how much Kara needed a male influence in her life. With her father gone and no family to speak of, there really hadn't been a male role model for Kara. Now it seemed that Noah had stepped into the position seamlessly, and Annie felt a tenderness growing inside her for him.

If there was one sure way to a mother's heart, it was for a man to take an interest in her child. But the moment that thought entered her mind, she frowned a bit. What if there was an ulterior motive to Noah's kindness? What if he was being attentive to Kara to get closer to Annie?

No.

If that had been his plan, she told herself, he wouldn't have waited six months to begin it. She glanced up from her desk to see Kara's pale blond head bent next to Noah's dark one over his desk. He was explaining subtraction in a patient voice and Kara was hanging on his every word.

Annie couldn't quite quell a rush of wishful thinking. Up until recently she'd avoided categorizing her boss as an attractive single man. She'd trained herself to pay no attention at all to Noah's immense sexual energy. After all, she was his employee. But the truth was, he fairly oozed sensuality when he walked into a room, and he had the ability to send a shiver along her spine with a glance.

All of which was just a little disconcerting to a woman who hadn't had a man in her life in six years.

"That's why," she muttered, keeping her voice a husky whisper as she typed up one of Noah's letters. "You've been too long on your own and now you're starting to daydream. Do yourself a favor and cut it out."

"Who are you talking to?"

Briefly, she closed her eyes and muffled a groan as Noah walked up to her desk. *Please God, he didn't hear me.*

"Oh, just talking to myself."

"About anything interesting?"

When she looked up at him, something inside her turned over in a slow, easy roll. "No," she lied, then looked past him for Kara. Her daughter was sitting in Noah's chair at his desk, still doing homework. "If she's bothering you…"

"Do I look like I'm bothered?"

"No," she admitted, sliding her gaze back to him. "You look like you're being nice."

"And this worries you?" One corner of his mouth lifted into a half smile.

Oh, yes, it really did, Annie thought. Because the kinder he was to Kara, the warmer Annie felt toward him.

"Should it?"

He perched on the edge of her desk and looked down at her. "Depends," he said, "on what exactly you're worried over. Me spending time with Kara, or the time I've been spending with you?"

"Well, that gets right to the point of things, doesn't it?" she asked quietly, so that her daughter couldn't overhear.

"I told you that you would always get honesty from me, Annie."

"You did," she agreed, still meeting his gaze. She wished she could read his thoughts in his eyes, but she knew, from long experience with the man, that he guarded what he was thinking very carefully. He had a perfect poker face, in fact. Annie had seen him use that talent to his advantage in negotiations on more than one occasion. He was able to get exactly what he wanted from his business opponent without giving away any more than he planned to.

But it was a different matter altogether having those cool, carefully shuttered eyes focused on her.

Wants she'd denied, desires she hadn't given thought to in years were suddenly racing through her mind, her body. So far, Annie hadn't been able to squash them.

Maybe it was time to try.

"So, Noah, being honest, why are you being so nice to us?" She was holding her breath as she waited for his answer and vaguely wondered if he could tell.

"Fair question," he said with a nod. "The honest answer is…I don't know."

A short laugh shot from her throat. Not what she'd expected, but somehow his answer made her feel less…uncomfortable. "Okay, that's honest."

He smiled at her. "I could say that I like your daughter, but then you'd worry that I was cultivating her to get close to you."

She flushed and he noticed.

"Already considered that, have you?"

"And dismissed it," she admitted. "As long as we're being honest, I did wonder. But if that was what you were up to, you would hardly have waited for months to try out your plan."

"Unless I'm diabolical."

Annie laughed again, as she was sure he'd meant her to.

"Look," he said, standing up from the desk and shoving his hands into his slacks pockets, "I don't have an ulterior motive in this. Kara was upset. It was easy enough to give her chores around here to help out."

"And the rides home every night?"

He shook his head. "You're really dissecting everything, aren't you?"

"I suppose I am," she said, giving her daughter another glance to make sure she was still in Noah's office and out of earshot.

"There's no ulterior motive," he told her again, his eyes locking with hers as if he was willing her to believe him. "But if you want to pay me back, make me dinner."

"Dinner?"

"Do I make you nervous?"

"Yes."

He grinned. "You don't have any reason to be."

"Yet somehow that changes nothing," she told him. Swarms of butterflies took off in the pit of her stomach. Her mouth went dry and her palms were damp. Being the sole focus of a man like Noah was enough to make any woman feel a little...out of her depth.

Yet at the same time there was a small thrill of excitement, edginess that she hadn't felt in far too long. And realizing that made her say honestly, "As flattered as I am, I'm not in a position to indulge myself in a flirtation with the boss, Noah."

"Who said anything about a flirtation?"

She shook her head. "Whatever it is you're hinting at, then. I have Kara to think about."

"It's just dinner, Annie."

Oh, it was much more than dinner, she thought, and she knew that he was aware of that fact, too. There was so much tension between them, she could hardly draw a breath. She was very much in danger of breaking her own solemn vow not to become involved with a man until Kara was older. And if she did, she could very well be risking the job she needed to keep the home they both loved.

But how could she say no to making him dinner when he'd been nothing but kind to both her and her daughter?

CHAPTER
∽FOUR∾

NOAH LOOKED AROUND the small, tidy kitchen and smiled to himself. Annie's house was just what he would have expected. A cottage, filled with homey furniture, colorful rugs and pillows and a sense of welcome that had reached out to him the moment he walked through the door.

"I hope spaghetti's okay," Annie was saying as Noah took a seat at the kitchen table.

"Sounds great," he said, shifting his gaze to the backyard, where Kara played on a swing set. "I like your house."

Annie laughed a little and gave the sauce another stir. "Thank you. It's small, but it's perfect for Kara and me."

It was small, he thought. He could probably fit the entire cottage inside his house three times over. His place was everything he'd once dreamed of owning. A showplace that proved to him he'd finally arrived. But somehow he'd never noticed that the big, expensive house was really pretty much an empty shell. It was nothing like this place, filled with warmth and life and— He cut that thought off fast. No point in being dissatisfied with the very thing you'd always wanted. But the sound of Kara's laughter spilling in from the yard put the lie to that.

He needed to turn his thoughts somewhere else. To focus on something other than the way Annie Moore looked as she stood at the stove in faded jeans, a T-shirt and bare feet. "So tell me about Kara's friend. The one who started this whole thing."

"Gracie," she said, moving to the refrigerator, where she pulled out a pitcher of iced tea. While she spoke, she set the pitcher on the table and went to get glasses. "As soon as we moved here, Gracie and Kara became instant friends. The kind of best friend you only seem to make when you're a child."

She smiled, poured them both tall glasses of tea then sat down opposite him. "Moving is hard on children, you uproot them from the familiar and settle them down in a place where they have to make new friends."

Noah knew all about that. He remembered all too well the anxiety of never knowing which day might be his last with his current "family." "Yeah," he said simply, "it can be tough."

Her eyes met his briefly, and he saw questions

written in their depths. He ignored them. "So Kara and Gracie became friends."

"Yes," she said, smiling again. "Every day after school it was 'Gracie said this. Gracie said that.' Then…" Annie sighed a little and cupped her hands around the glass. "Before we moved here, I knew all of Kara's friends. But since coming to Crescent Bay, I've been so busy trying to get us both settled into our new life, I haven't had the time—" She broke off and shook her head. "No. I haven't made the time to get to know our neighbors and the kids at the school. If I had, I might have seen this coming. Because, Kara being who she is, I'm not surprised at all that she decided to 'fix' Gracie's problems herself. That's what best friends do, isn't it?"

"I suppose," he said, enjoying the ease between them. Truthfully, he was enjoying being here, in this warm kitchen with a pretty woman opposite him and a child playing in the yard.

Strange, but in the years since he'd set out to make his fortune, he'd never really taken the time to realize what he'd been giving up by being so solitary. He'd been so attentive to his career, to the life he'd wanted to build for himself, that he'd never noticed that the luxurious world he'd constructed was an empty one.

"Mrs. Higgins—at the shoe store—" Annie qualified.

"I know who she is."

She nodded. "When I took Kara there for her to apologize, Mrs. Higgins told me that there were other children in town doing without decent shoes. Apparently Gracie isn't alone in this. And I just..."

"You just what?"

She turned her head to look at her daughter shooting down the slide. "I hate to think that there are children out there with no one to help them. I hate thinking about parents who are forced to make their children do without."

"Sometimes," he said quietly, "there's nothing you can do about the problem. Sometimes a thing just is."

"I don't believe that." She whirled back to look at him, her gaze meeting his almost defiantly. "And I don't think you do, either. If you did, you wouldn't have given Kara a chance to earn the money to buy those shoes."

"That was different. That was helping a little girl who was crying. I can't change the world, Annie. Neither can you. And if you try, you'll only end up breaking your own heart."

"If everyone felt that way, nothing would ever be solved."

He shook his head and leaned back in his chair. "I admire the fire behind the words," he said, couching his own words carefully. "But you don't know what it's like. A new pair of shoes isn't going to make a big enough difference in a child's life to worry about. Their families will still be struggling. They might still be hungry. What does a new pair of shoes change?"

"Everything," she said, and he could literally see

the sparks of challenge dazzling her eyes. "Kara said the other kids made fun of Gracie."

"Kids are cruel," he pointed out.

"Yes, unfortunately they are. But don't you see, when Gracie gets those shoes, there'll be nothing obvious for the other children to make fun of. She'll be happier. More alert. More confident. She'll go to her classes with her head held high and…"

"And what?" he asked, leaning toward her over the table. "Grow up to be president, all because of a new pair of shoes?"

"Maybe." Her features went stiff and her eyes flashed. "Why not?"

"Don't you get it? It's not that easy."

"I didn't say it was easy," she told him quietly.

Noah knew he should shut up now. Just drop this whole conversation, but damned if he could stop the words from pouring from his throat. "A pair of shoes won't feed a kid. Won't make him feel wanted. Or needed. It won't change his life."

"It could change the way that child feels about himself, and sometimes I think that's enough."

He scrubbed one hand across the back of his neck and took a long drink of his iced tea.

"Noah…" She reached out, laid one hand over his and asked, "Who are we talking about now? Gracie? Or you?"

He laughed harshly, a scrape of sound against his throat. In the past few days he'd unwillingly done more thinking about his own past than he had in years. And of course his memories were getting in

the way, coloring his reactions. He'd never told anyone else about his childhood, but looking into Annie's eyes, he let the words come.

"Got me. Okay, yeah. I know what it's like for
Gracie and the other kids like her. Hell, they've probably got it better than I did. I was a foster kid," he
said, sliding his hand from beneath hers, despite
missing the warmth of her touch almost instantly.
He stood and walked across the small kitchen. Standing at the counter, he stared out the window at the
yard and the gathering dusk. It was easier than meeting Annie's eyes as he tore open an old wound. "I
know all about old clothes, hand-me-down shoes that
don't fit. Everything I had was donated by someone,
somewhere, to the county. And nothing changed for
me until I changed it."

He hated remembering what it had been like to
be a child powerless to help himself. He hated the
shame of knowing what he wore was ill fitted and
old. Maybe that was why the situation with Kara
had hit him so hard. Had drawn him in so quickly.
So deeply.

A long-buried part of him was standing up, de-
manding to be recognized.

"And you had no help at all?"

Blowing out a breath, Noah looked out at Kara,
swinging now, shooting her little legs out and up to
the sky as if half expecting to actually fly. "There
were a couple of families who tried, yes. But it didn't
make a difference."

"Are you sure?" Annie stood up, too, and walked

toward him. He heard her footsteps on the linoleum and turned his head to look at her, bracing himself for pity he didn't want.

But she surprised him. She didn't offer sympathy.

"Could it be that maybe those families who tried are what gave you the determination to succeed?" she asked and waited until he looked at her before continuing. Her eyes were sharp and clear, without the shadow of pity. "What if it was those people who fed your confidence enough so that you believed you could make something of yourself?"

Noah hadn't really considered it before, but he supposed it might be true. A couple of times as a child, he'd worn new clothing. New shoes. And he had felt different. He'd felt as if he belonged. As if he were just like every other kid. And as he realized it, he looked at Annie and nodded slowly.

"All right, maybe you've got a point." He turned his back on the window, leaned against the counter and folded his arms across his chest. "I hadn't thought of it like that because, frankly, I'd rather not remember that time at all."

"That's a shame," she said.

He laughed shortly. "Would you want to remember?"

"It would be hard to ignore a part of what made me who I am today." She shook her head and added, "I had a family. A nice home. So maybe I can't understand what you went through. What kids like Gracie are going through now. But everyone has problems, Noah. No one gets through life walking under a rainbow. We all have things we'd rather not think about or dwell on. It's what we do with our lives in spite of those memories that counts."

"You make it sound so simple."

"Oh, it's not," she allowed with a rueful smile. She turned her gaze out on her daughter and sighed a little. "When Kara's dad died, I was terrified. I was alone with a baby to take care of. Those days can still come back to haunt me," she added as she looked up at him again. "But I made it through. We made it through. And we've got a nice life now. Isn't that what matters most?"

"Yeah. Yeah, it is." Noah nodded thoughtfully. He had shared things with her that he'd never told anyone else. He was feeling something for her that he'd never known before and he realized that for him, there would be no going back. "You know, Annie Moore, you're really an amazing woman."

She smiled at him. "Noah Fielding, are you flirting with me?"

A tight, cold band around his heart loosened as he admitted, "Looks like I am. What do you think about that?"

She gave him a slow smile. "I think I like it."

"WHAT'S THIS?" NOAH came up behind her desk the following afternoon and looked over her shoulder at her computer screen.

A bubble of excitement danced through Annie as she turned her face up to his. "I found this website online. It's for an organization called Shoes That Fit.

They're in Claremont—just a couple of hours from here." She looked back at the screen, at the flashing images of smiling children. "This whole situation with Kara and Gracie and the new shoes has had me thinking for days about possibilities. After all, it's not just the O'Malley family having trouble. A lot of people around here are."

"Yeah, I know," he said.

"Well, look what I found."

"Shoes That Fit," Noah mused, leaning over her for a better look at the screen. "They donate shoes to kids in need?"

"Not just shoes, but backpacks filled with school supplies," Annie told him. "And school uniforms. Pretty much everything a child needs to feel confidence in himself."

She reached for his hand and held on. "I called them while you were on that conference call with the lawyer. I actually spoke to the executive director, Roni Lomeli, and she was terrific. She told me so many wonderful stories about how they've helped children in hundreds of communities in California. And it's all done in a way that not only saves face for the kids' families, but for the kids themselves. Oh, Noah. Just listening to her, I wanted to rush right out and make the kind of difference she has."

He eased back and sat on the corner of her desk. "You've really given this a lot of thought."

"I really have. And talking to Roni just sort of solidified everything for me. You know, this organization helped more than one hundred thousand children last year in dozens of states. That's amazing. It shows what can happen, how change can ripple out from one person helping another." Annie looked up into his eyes and said, "Going over this website, reading the thank-you letters from children whose lives have been changed, has really motivated me, Noah. We could do this. Here. In Crescent Bay. We could help by starting our own Shoes That Fit chapter right here."

Noah smiled at her and stroked the back of her hand with his thumb. "I'm guessing you've got a plan."

She grinned. "Just the start of one. It's going to take some refining." Turning back to study the bright, cheerful website, she admitted, "But the Shoes That Fit organization is really helpful, and they'll go out of their way to assist us if we're interested in starting up a chapter."

"We?"

Annie heard the questions tucked into that one word and held her breath as she looked back at him. His features gave away nothing of what he was thinking. She couldn't tell if he was amused or irritated. If he was going to be the Noah she'd come to know and care for—or if he was going to retreat into the too-private, distant man she'd always thought him to be.

She held her breath, hoping that he wouldn't pull back. Wouldn't turn from this. From her.

"I thought," she said slowly, "that with your help, it would all go much faster."

"Is that the only reason you want me involved?"

"What other reason is there?" she asked, refusing to admit to wanting him as her partner in this until she knew how he felt, too.

As if understanding exactly what she was thinking, he stood, pulled her to her feet and tipped her chin up with his fingertips. His gaze locked with hers, and Annie felt heat sweep through her. His eyes weren't distant and cold. Instead, they were shining down at her with all the warmth she'd ever dreamed of.

"Do I really need to tell you the other reason?" he asked.

"No," she said with a slight shake of her head. "No, you really don't. But you could show me."

Smiling, he dipped his head to hers and kissed her, a delicate, gentle brush of his lips to hers. And it was enough to send sparks dazzling through her system.

Here, she thought, *is everything I'd hoped to find.*

When she opened her eyes to look up at him, his gaze moved over her face as tenderly as a touch might have.

"I think, Annie Moore," he whispered, "we're destined to be a great team."

CHAPTER
⟶FIVE⟶

NOAH SAT AT his desk the following afternoon and marveled at the changes in his life over the past week. He never would have believed that anyone's world could transform so completely in so little time. But maybe, he thought, it was because he'd been ready for it, whether he'd known it or not.

From the outer office came the sound of something crashing to the floor. Noah grinned.

"Sorry!" Kara's voice was singsongy as she picked up her mother's desk phone from the floor, where she'd knocked it in her dusting efforts.

"Are you all right?" Since Annie was downstairs at the mall, taking today's mail to the post office, he and Kara were alone in the office.

"I'm fine. I knocked the phone off the desk."

"Again," he said when she stuck her head around the door to give him an impish grin.

"Again," she agreed, pushing strands of blond hair out of her eyes.

Noah had never really cared for children much, but being around Kara had opened his eyes to what he'd been missing. It had opened his heart to the possibilities that existed if he would just reach out for them.

"I'm all done, Noah," Kara announced as she walked into his office and leaned on his desk.

"You must be pretty close to being able to buy Gracie's shoes by now, aren't you?"

She walked around the edge of his desk, trailing slightly grubby fingers across its surface. "After you pay me today, I can buy them," she said proudly. "Then Gracie can go on the field trip with me on Friday and nobody will laugh at her ever again."

The heart that had so recently been awakened inside Noah's chest ached a bit—with pride, with love—for the shining little girl looking up at him with adoration in her eyes. A hell of a responsibility, he thought, accepting a child's love. And he made a promise to himself never to let her down.

"You've done good work here this week, Kara," he told her as he reached into his wallet for a five-dollar bill. "I'm proud of you."

Her grin brightened even further. "You wanna help me count the money?"

Amused, he asked, "Don't you already know how much is in your safe box?"

"Yeah, but it's fun to count it!" Without waiting for a response, she raced out to her mother's desk, sneakers slapping against the floor in her rush. In a blink she was back, setting the small wooden box on his desk.

"Here's your pay for today," he said. She nipped it from his fingers. Then she opened the box reverently, looked inside and went perfectly still. "It's gone."

"What?" He sat up, looked into the box and saw she was right. It was empty.

The little girl turned big blue eyes swimming with tears up to him. "Noah, where'd it go? Gracie's shoe money's all gone and I worked so hard and now I can't get the shoes and Gracie won't be able to go on the field trip with me. Noah, where is it?"

"I don't know, sweetie," he said, irritation spiking inside him. Annie wouldn't have moved the money without telling her daughter. And he hadn't done it. The only other explanation was that someone had stolen it.

Instinct had him pulling the crying little girl into his arms. She cuddled against him and sobbed, her body shaking with the force of her tears and crushing hurt.

"Did somebody take it, do you think?" She asked her question between hiccupping sobs. "Who would do it? Why would they do it?"

"I don't know, sweetie, but I'll find out," he promised. He pulled her up onto his lap, and when she curled into him for comfort, the last, lingering trace of the "old" Noah faded away. He wasn't the man he'd been. Now he was the man who loved a child and her mother. The man who would make this right for Kara.

"Are you sure you didn't take the money home with you last night?" he asked quietly.

She shook her head against him, burrowing closer. "Uh-uh. Remember, we went to the pizza place before you took us home and I told you I almost had enough money for the shoes so I was gonna keep it in Mommy's desk so I could go and buy them right away. And now it's all gone!"

"It'll be all right, Kara," he murmured.

When the office door opened and Annie walked in, he lifted his gaze to hers.

Annie was spellbound by the sight of Noah comforting her crying daughter. Her heart took that last wild leap into love. Hugging the knowledge to herself, she hurried across the room and asked, "What happened?"

In between sobs, her voice muffled against Noah's broad chest, Kara told her everything, and Annie's heart broke for her little girl. "I'm so sorry, baby."

Kara lifted her head from Noah's chest. Her eyes were red and her cheeks tearstained. "I get it now, Mommy. Why it's bad to steal. 'Cause this feels really, really bad inside."

"I know, honey." Annie smoothed her daughter's hair back from her face, then glanced at Noah.

"I can't buy Gracie's shoes now, Mommy," Kara said on a wail, dropping her face back to Noah's chest.

"Yes, you can," he told her, shifting her slightly

so that he could look into her bereft eyes. "I'm going to replace the money you lost and then we're going shopping."

"You are?" Kara blinked up at him, hope beginning to shine in her features.

"Noah, you don't have to do that," Annie told him with a shake of her head. "I'll give Kara the money and—"

"No. Her money was stolen from my office, so I'll make it good. And I'll find out who took it. But that's for later." His gaze met Annie's. "I'm not going to let a thief steal Kara's dream. Not when she's worked so hard for it."

Annie took a breath and held it. He cared. For her. For Kara. And that was such a gift she hardly knew what to say. But her daughter didn't seem to have that trouble.

"You can't buy the shoes, Noah," she said softly. "Not you, either, Mommy. I have to buy them for a present. Because if a grown-up buys them, then Gracie might get embarrassed and I don't want her to feel bad."

"I am so proud of you," Annie said.

"You're a very special little girl," Noah told her, "and Gracie's lucky to have you as a friend. But, Kara, I'm not buying the shoes. You are. It's your money. You worked for it. I'm just giving you back what was stolen. Do you understand?"

She thought about that for a long minute, chewing at her bottom lip. "I guess that's okay, then. Is it, Mommy?"

"I think," Annie said, looking directly into Noah's eyes, "that it's absolutely perfect."

He smiled at both of them. "Now that that's settled, I think there's a little girl who needs to buy her friend some shoes."

"Now?" Kara asked. "Really?"

"Right now," he said, smiling. He took out his wallet, counted the money into Kara's waiting hand and asked, "Well? Ready to go shopping?"

Clutching the money in one tight fist, Kara threw her arms around his neck and said, "You should have a little girl, Noah, because you'd be a good daddy."

"You think so?"

"Uh-huh."

Annie inhaled sharply and felt the sting of tears in her own eyes. Her daughter, whether she'd said so or not, was coming to love Noah Fielding. And now, looking into Noah's eyes, Annie saw that the feeling was mutual. It seemed as though this was all moving so quickly. And yet, on another level, she felt as though she'd known Noah forever. Now, as she looked into his eyes, she saw the promise of something wonderful written there.

Idly she wondered if she would have a nameless thief to thank for one of the most beautiful moments of her life.

KARA HUGGED THE shoe box to her chest throughout the ride to Gracie O'Malley's house. The smile on her face was bright as sunlight and her eyes were clear and shining with happiness, her earlier misery forgotten in the anticipation of giving something important to a friend she loved.

Noah looked at her in the rearview mirror and knew he'd never enjoyed a shopping trip more. Watching the little girl proudly march into Mrs. Higgins's shoe store and pay for something she'd worked so hard for was...more touching than he would have imagined.

Glancing at Annie in the passenger seat beside him, he noted her smile, too, and realized that somehow over the past week or so, Annie Moore and her daughter had become not just important to him, but essential.

Not so long ago, that thought would have given him plenty to worry about. Now he was wise enough to be grateful for whatever fates had conspired to bring the three of them together.

"There it is!" Kara shouted from the backseat. "That's Gracie's house! Look! She's right there in the yard with her brother and sister!"

"Okay, we'll park and then—"

"Not in front of her house, okay?" Kara spoke up quickly, practically bouncing in her seat. "I don't want her to know you guys are watching, 'cause she might get all embarrassed and stuff, okay?"

He glanced at Annie, and at her nod, Noah pulled to the curb two houses up from the O'Malley place.

The three of them got out of the car, but Kara could hardly stand still. "I want to go by myself, Mommy," she said, tightly clutching the shoe box.

"We'll wait for you right here, honey," Annie said, ruffling her daughter's bangs.

"Okay!" Grinning, Kara turned, ran a couple of steps then stopped and glanced back at them. "Thank you," she said, and took off running again, her small sneakers slapping against the sidewalk.

As he stood beside Annie in the shade of an old maple tree, Noah took a good look at the O'Malley house. Toys were scattered across the lawn and three kids were arguing over a bicycle. Small but neat, the house needed painting, but the yard was cared for and the porch swept. There was pride in that, he thought, and wondered about Gracie's father. Had he lost his job? What was the source of their troubles? The fact that he not only wondered but cared was a sort of miracle to him.

Noah felt as if Annie and Kara had opened up a new world to him. But the reality was, he admitted ruefully, they were simply bringing him back to life.

"She's great, you know?" he said, experiencing a swell of pride as Kara stopped outside the O'Malleys' front gate. "She's not interested in thanks or even in hearing from us that she's doing a nice thing. All she cares about is her friend." He shook his head in amazement. "When I was a kid, I was sometimes on the receiving end of 'good works.' Trust me when I say most people prefer taking a bow when they do something nice."

She tipped her head to one side. "You're here and not taking a bow."

Noah nodded. "True. But I'm here with you. Because of you. You and Kara."

"The reason doesn't matter." She looked briefly toward her daughter. "But you're right about Kara. She has a big heart, but even knowing that, kids can really amaze you. They feel so much and notice so much more than you think they do."

"You know, in the past week I've had my eyes opened about a few things."

"Is that right?" she asked.

Nodding, he stared off down the street at the children playing in the yard. "This thing with the shoes for Gracie has really gotten to me. The chapter of Shoes That Fit you wanted to open? It's a great idea, Annie. I think we could make a real difference in Crescent Bay."

"I think you're right."

"But this isn't just about what we're going to build here in town together." He watched as a slight breeze lifted her hair from her collar and tossed it gently around her face. "I want you to know that I'm interested in more than working with you."

"Noah…"

He shook his head, dropped one arm around her shoulders and pulled her close to his side. "You don't have to say anything. Not yet. There's no rush, Annie. For either of us. But you should know that now that I've found you and Kara, I'm not going to let you go."

She leaned into him, laid her head on his shoulder and sighed a little. "We're not going to let you go, either, Noah. Neither of us is."

"Good to know." Noah grinned, hugged her hard and dropped a kiss onto her forehead. Then together they turned to watch the small drama unfold.

As Kara approached the front gate, a little red-haired girl rushed across the lawn to meet her.

"Gracie, I presume," he said.

"That's her." Annie leaned into Noah as they watched Kara talking excitedly before handing the shoe box over the top of the gate to her friend.

Gracie accepted the box as if it was made of spun glass. With a broad smile, she smoothed her small hands across the box lid over and over again, as if she couldn't quite believe she was actually touching it.

They couldn't hear what was said, but for this interaction, words were unnecessary.

"Is she ever going to open the box?" Noah asked.

"She's getting to it," Annie told him, sniffling a little as Gracie's brother and sister came closer and the gate swung open so that Kara could slip inside.

A solitary tear rolling down Annie's cheek clutched at Noah's heart. An understanding smile on his face, he reached into his slacks pocket and produced a handkerchief. "Now I know why I carry these things," he said, handing it to her.

"My hero." She dried her eyes, laughed a little and leaned into him again, as if needing the closeness as much as he did.

"Look," he said, giving her a one-armed hug. "She's finally opening the box."

Gracie grinned as she pulled the new shoes free and immediately sat down on the grass to put them on. When the laces were tied, she stood up gingerly, as if half-afraid to get the new soles dirty. Then Kara laughed and reached out for her hand. Gracie grabbed it and both girls jumped up and down in delight.

The O'Malleys' front door opened and a couple stepped onto the porch. Gracie ran to them, quickly showed off her new sneakers then dashed back to the gate and her friend.

From their vantage point in the shadows Noah and Annie looked on as Gracie's father wrapped his arm around his wife's waist and the two of them smiled, watching their daughter and her friend. The girls had raced to the sidewalk to compare their matching shoes. And in the deepening twilight, Gracie's new sneakers glittered and shone with the magic of Cinderella's glass slippers.

As the girls skipped along the sidewalk, hand in hand, giving those sneakers a trial run, Noah rested his chin atop Annie's head.

"Thank you," he whispered.

"For what?"

"For this," he told her, his voice raw with the wealth of emotion clogging his throat. "For letting me be a part of this. For reminding me what it's like to be a kid with few options."

"Noah…"

He held her tighter to him. "For so long I've spent every minute concentrating on building my own security, my own little empire. And I'd forgotten that sometimes a new pair of shoes is more important than anything."

Annie tipped her head back to look up at him and he lost himself for a moment or two in the tear-washed shine of her eyes.

"Did you see what happened to Gracie when she put those sneakers on?" He pulled in a deep breath. "She stood taller somehow." Noah turned Annie in his arms, holding her close. "Kara gave her more than a pair of shoes, Annie. She gave her confidence. Let her know that she's important to someone. That she matters."

He smiled then and shook his head. "In the past week or so, you and Kara have managed to show me what my life was lacking. What I'd set aside in my rush to succeed."

"Tell me," she coaxed, reaching up to cup his cheek in the palm of her hand.

He felt the warmth of her touch slip deep inside him, chasing away the remaining dregs of cold and shadows he'd been carrying with him for years. "You two reminded me that all the security in the world doesn't mean a thing if you're alone. If you have no one to share it with. And you taught me just how right it feels when you do something really good for someone else. When you make a difference in someone's life."

Annie laughed a little and shook her head as she stared up at him. "Noah, we didn't give you anything you didn't already have. It's because of you that Kara was able to give her friend those shoes. You took the time to see what Kara needed and you found a way to help her earn that gift."

He grinned down at her and felt like a king. Lifting his gaze to where the two little girls were laughing and talking beside the O'Malleys' front gate, he said, "So about that chapter of Shoes That Fit..."

"Yes..."

"Nothing's stopping us from getting started on that right away, is there?"

"There's really not," she said, moving in for a kiss as the laughter of two little girls carried through the evening breeze.

CHAPTER
⌁—SIX—⌁

FOR THE NEXT COUPLE of months, Annie worked with
Shoes That Fit as she and Noah went about setting up
their local chapter. While the paperwork was being
done, Annie did some research and talked to the
principals of the local schools. There were so many
kids who needed help. At night, she and Noah would
go over ideas and plans.

They started out small, setting up donation jars
in the stores at the mall. Money began to trickle in
as word spread, and the donations began to mount.
Annie was astounded by the generosity of the people
in town, but the contributions that most touched her
heart came from the children.

Boys and girls readily gave their allowances.
Some kids carried in piggy banks stuffed with
change and handed them over with smiles on their

faces. Gracie and Kara collected cans, took them to the recycling center and donated their proceeds.

It was as if the community had come together, now that they knew a problem existed, to help all of the town's children. Annie felt as though she was in the middle of a whirlwind because everything was happening so fast.

And it wasn't only her chapter of Shoes That Fit that was developing so quickly. In the past two months she and Noah had forged such a close relationship, working together so smoothly, so effortlessly, it was as if they'd been somehow meant to find each other. To make each other whole and then help spread that sense of completeness. It was exciting and somehow fulfilling to work in tandem on a project that involved the whole community.

Noah loved her. She knew it even though he'd yet to say the words. And she was sure of her own feelings, as well. Annie smiled to herself as she realized that Kara had already pretty much adopted Noah as her own, so there was no trouble there, either. But even as she considered all of this, she had to acknowledge that nothing had been said about the future, and she couldn't help wondering if there was going to be one for them.

After all, love didn't necessarily translate into marriage and family and happily ever after for everyone. Just because she hungered for those things with Noah didn't mean he shared those feelings. Was she just setting herself up for heartbreak somewhere down the road? Should she do the smart thing and protect herself?

Or was it too late for that already?

"Yes, it is," she confessed in a barely heard whisper. She was in love and there was no going back. Noah held her heart, and there was no way now to pull back from the situation that had come on her out of nowhere.

Her first marriage had been a slow and steady building of feelings. And if Kara's father had lived, she would have stayed with him happily, never knowing that there was so much more to be experienced.

What she and Noah shared had blossomed and grown so quickly, she'd been swept off her feet before she could even realize what was happening. And, she told herself, she wouldn't have had it any other way.

Smiling to herself, Annie took a deep breath and let worry drop from her shoulders. Whatever happened between her and Noah would take care of itself eventually.

But meanwhile they each had new obligations to consider. Contributions to their new project were being tallied daily.

Now they were expanding their efforts, not just accepting monetary contributions but following the guide in the Shoes That Fit start-up kit; people could buy shoes for specific children. That way, they could feel a connection to a child in need and know that they were making a personal difference.

It had been only two months since all of this had

begun, but now a brightly painted kiosk stood in the middle of Fielding Center Mall.

Annie stood nearby and watched people as they approached it curiously, reading the boldly lettered sign: Shoes That Fit—Best Foot Forward Chapter. She and Noah together had come up with the name for their community project, and thought it represented exactly what they were trying to get across— that with new shoes, children gained confidence and were able to put their best foot forward because they felt as though they belonged. They weren't ashamed or worried about how they would look to the other children. And without the worries of social judgments raining down on them, they could concentrate on their schoolwork.

"Looks good," Noah said, coming up behind her.

"It does." Annie glanced over her shoulder at him and smiled. "I saw the ad in the paper this morning. Very cleverly done."

He winked. "My new marketing executive came up with the idea."

Annie grinned. Just another reason for her to love Noah Fielding. Kevin O'Malley, Gracie's father, had started his new job with Fielding Enterprises only a few days ago and already had come up with some brilliant plans. "Gracie got a new pair of shoes and her father found a job."

Noah shrugged and took her hand in his. "Only made sense. After I found out that Kevin had been laid off from a marketing firm in San Francisco, I realized he'd be perfect for my company."

There was more to it than that, of course, Annie thought. Kevin O'Malley had lost his job and then he and his wife had lost the house they'd owned in San Francisco. They'd moved here, to Crescent Bay, to live in his wife's mother's house. They were eager to rebuild the savings they'd lost when the bottom had dropped out of their world.

Which, Annie told herself, just went to prove that hard times hit every level of society. It wasn't only the desperately poor who needed occasional help. Sometimes the middle class fell between the cracks when hit by misfortune.

"I'd say Kevin's starting off great," Noah said, staring at the kiosk surrounded by curious shoppers. "Aside from all the interesting ideas he's come up with for Fielding Enterprises, that ad he designed for the paper and the TV and radio ads he talked me into have really sparked interest in Shoes That Fit."

"It was a nice thing you did, Noah, hiring Kevin."

He shook his head. "He's a good worker. And more, after seeing how his daughter reacted to the shoes Kara bought for her, he's as committed to this project as we are."

True. Thanks to the measuring charts and forms from the Shoes That Fit kit, schoolteachers and nurses had been able to surreptitiously gather information on the children who needed help and determine their shoe sizes. Without revealing the children's names, index cards containing that information were hung in the kiosk that Annie and Noah were still observing with satisfaction.

"Mrs. Higgins is doing a booming business these days, too," Annie said with a quick glance toward the shoe store where Kara's "adventure" had started. People were streaming in and out of the tidy shop, carrying boxes of shoes to the drop-off point managed by several mall employees.

"That was Kevin's idea, too," Noah told her. "Customers who go to her store with an index card and buy a pair of shoes for a child in need get half off on any other pair."

"With you making up the difference for her," Annie reminded him, knowing that Noah had guaranteed Mrs. Higgins wouldn't lose money by being the focus of this fund-raiser.

Noah only shrugged. "It's good business. The mall's crowded, store owners are happy and the kids are getting what they need."

He could brush off her pride all he wanted, but Annie knew the truth. Noah was making this work, and she loved him for it—and for so many other reasons she couldn't even name them all.

"You're doing a terrific thing here," she said.

"No, we are. And our chapter of Shoes That Fit is off to a great start." He took her hand and walked toward the kiosk, where several shoppers were choosing index cards. "Of course, when the donated shoes start piling up, things are going to get crazy."

A FEW DAYS LATER Noah remembered what he'd said to Annie and figured it had to be the biggest understatement in the history of the world.

Throughout his office and Annie's, shoe boxes were stacked everywhere. Towers of brightly colored boxes in different sizes took up most of the room. Noah was amazed at people's generosity. The first batch of index-card wish lists was completed, which meant that children the most desperately in need were about to receive brand-new shoes.

The driver he'd hired to make the deliveries was efficiently carrying stacks of boxes to the truck downstairs. Meanwhile, Annie and Kara were busily taping corresponding index cards to the appropriate shoe boxes so that they'd be easily distributed at the schools.

He leaned against the doorjamb leading into his private office and watched as Kara happily neglected her taping job, moving curiously from box to box to peek inside at all the different shoes.

That one little girl had started all of this, he mused, just because she'd wanted to help her friend. Love had begun it, he realized, and love would complete it.

A few months ago he'd hardly known Kara—beyond being aware of her existence, of course. Now he couldn't imagine not having that laughing, amazing little girl in his life.

As for her mother…hard to believe he'd spent six months ignoring her. Impossible to believe that he'd managed it.

Noah's gaze fixed on Annie as she flashed a smile at her daughter and finished taping an index card to a bright pink box. He hadn't been looking for love. Hadn't thought he wanted, or needed it. Now nothing mattered more than Annie.

Odd how quickly and completely a man's world could change for the better.

"Mommy!" Kara cooed the word as she opened yet another box. "There's blue tennies in this one. Can I have blue tennies, too?"

"We'll see…." She turned to help the driver gather up another load of boxes for his next trip down to the truck. When he was gone, her gaze landed on Noah observing her from the doorway. "Noah? Is everything all right?"

He smiled. "Why wouldn't it be?"

She sighed, looked around at the small mountain of shoe boxes and laughed. "Well, we're a little crazed at the moment."

"Yeah, we are." He wove his way past piles of boxes to get to her side, then reached down, took her hands and drew her to her feet.

"I haven't gotten to your correspondence yet," she confessed, and glanced at her desk, also covered with shoe boxes. "It probably won't go out until tomorrow."

"Doesn't matter," he said.

She tipped her head to one side, gave him a smile and asked, "Is this the same Noah Fielding I came to work for?"

"No," he said solemnly. "I'm not that Noah Fielding anymore. Thanks to you. And Kara."

"Are you sure you're okay?" she asked, apparently picking up on his seriousness.

"I'm good, Annie." He turned and waved a hand, indicating the boxes filling the room. "But I've realized that this is just the beginning. There are still kids out there who need shoes. And doesn't Shoes That Fit also provide things like backpacks with school supplies, too?"

"Yes, but—"

"No buts," he said, smiling down into her eyes and sensing his whole world settle around him. As it had been meant to, he acknowledged, from the moment he'd first laid eyes on Annie Moore. A part of him had known all along what she was. Who she was. Which was probably why he'd done his best to ignore her and what she made him feel.

Well, those days were gone. And he was grateful.

"We've started something here, Annie," he told her. "Something that's going to grow far beyond just us and our community."

"I hope so, Noah," she said.

"We've got a lot of work ahead of us." Noah shot a look at Kara, who gave him a wide, gap-toothed grin as she walked to join them. "All three of us. And that's what I want to talk to you about."

Annie nodded and chewed at her bottom lip as if she was nervous. Well, he wasn't. He'd spent years avoiding commitments of any kind. Now he thought nothing was more important than belonging with this woman and her daughter. Noah had never been so sure of anything in his life. He knew exactly what he wanted, and he would do anything necessary to get it.

"Before the truck driver comes back for the next load, I wanted to tell you something. Both of you."

"Me, too?" Kara asked, leaning against him as she turned her face up to his.

"Yes," he said, bending to lift Kara up and hold her in the crook of one arm. With his free hand he reached for Annie's hand and, holding it tightly, he looked into her blue eyes and said, "My life is full now because of you and Kara. The two of you have given me more than I ever thought possible."

"Oh, Noah…" Annie gulped in a breath and Kara wrapped one arm around his neck.

"What'd we give you, Noah?" Kara asked.

He laughed and said, "I'll tell you someday, sweetie."

Noah felt better than he ever had and knew that now was the time to ask the question that would settle their futures forever.

"Standing here," he said, "in the middle of something we created together, I want to ask you to marry me, Annie. I want us, the three of us, to be a family. And to help each other. To start more chapters of Shoes That Fit in other communities to help them, too."

"Oh, my." She was smiling and crying at the same time. His heart gave a hard lurch.

"Don't cry, Mommy," Kara said softly.

"It's happy crying, baby," she whispered.

He laughed aloud. "Marry me, Annie," he said again. "With my two best girls by my side, I know the three of us can do anything."

"Noah…" She lifted one hand to her mouth and shook her head. "I don't even know what to say."

"Say yes. Just say yes, Annie."

"I do love you," she told him, "but this isn't just about me, Noah. Kara and I are a team. We both have to be happy with this decision. So it's not just me who owes you an answer."

Nodding, he looked into the eyes of the little girl who'd first reminded him he had a heart, then had stolen it completely. "What do you say, Kara? Would you like to be my little girl? Will you let me be your dad?"

Kara looked from Noah to her mother and back again. Finally she smiled, cupped his cheeks in her small hands and said, "Well, you do need a little girl and I need a daddy—and maybe a sister."

Annie laughed and Noah grinned at the girl in his arms. "I'll see what I can do."

Nodding thoughtfully, Kara said simply, "Then I think we should get married." Smiling, she added, "Can I get some blue tennies before we go home?"

* * * * *

Dear Reader,

I was very honored when Marsha Zinberg called and invited me to participate in the *More Than Words* collection. Harlequin's dedication to showcasing women who do all they can to make the world a better place is a wonderful thing. In supporting these women and the organizations they represent, Harlequin highlights the best of all of us.

Like many other people, I get so involved in my own life—family, writing, the business of running a home—I sometimes forget to look up and around. To see what is happening not only in my community, but in my country. Researching Shoes That Fit changed all of that for me.

Can you imagine being a child whose only school shoes belonged to an older sibling? The shoes don't fit. They fall off. The other children laugh at your personal humiliation. How is a child supposed to concentrate on learning when they're too embarrassed to lift their heads up?

Shoes That Fit was founded in California in 1992 by Elodie McGuirk with the express purpose of providing all children with the simple yet priceless gift of new shoes. Since then, the organization has grown to sweep across our nation. Local chapters are run by volunteers, and now Shoes That Fit not only provides shoes for children in need, but new clothing, as well.

When I spoke with Roni Lomeli, the executive director of Shoes That Fit, I was impressed with her passion for what she does. Roni and her staff provide amazing help for the most deserving and the sometimes most overlooked segment of our citizens—our children.

I'd like to personally thank Roni for all she's done for our nation's children. And thank you, too, to Harlequin, for acknowledging her with this honor. Last, a big thank-you to you, the reader, for buying this book and doing your part to support these wonderful people.

I'm proud to be associated with this collection and I invite all of you readers to visit the website www.shoesthatfit.org to see how you can make a difference in a child's life.

All my best,
Maureen Child